PUFFIN BOOKS

WHAT A WEEK
TO FALL IN LOVE

'Mum! I'm not a kid any more – I don't want to celebrate my birthday with my *parents*, for heaven's sake! Get real!'

Her mother raised an eyebrow, which should have been a warning to Holly. She, however, was too irate to notice.

'And anyway, you can't do this to me because Dad said I could have a party!' she shouted. 'What's more, he said I could invite loads of friends – he PROMISED!'

What a Week to Fall in Love

Rosie Rushton

PUFFIN BOOKS

For the budding authors of
Mereway Middle School
who inspired more than
they know!

PUFFIN BOOKS

Published by the Penguin Group
Penguin Books Ltd, 27 Wrights Lane, London W8 5TZ, England
Penguin Putnam Inc., 375 Hudson Street, New York, New York 10014, USA
Penguin Books Australia Ltd, Ringwood, Victoria, Australia
Penguin Books Canada Ltd, 10 Alcorn Avenue, Toronto, Ontario, Canada M4V 3B2
Penguin Books (NZ) Ltd, 182–190 Wairau Road, Auckland 10, New Zealand

Penguin Books Ltd, Registered Offices: Harmondsworth, Middlesex, England

First published 1998
3 5 7 9 10 8 6 4 2

Copyright © Rosie Rushton, 1998
All rights reserved

The moral right of the author has been asserted

Set in Monotype Baskerville by
Rowland Phototypesetting Limited, Bury St Edmunds, Suffolk

Made and printed in England by Clays Ltd, St Ives plc

British Library Cataloguing in Publication Data
A CIP catalogue record for this book is
available from the British Library

ISBN 0-140-38760-9

MONDAY

7 a.m. 15 September. The Cedars,
Weston Way, West Green, Dunchester.
Despairing of mothers

Monday mornings, thought Holly Vine, yawning and flicking her nutmeg-brown hair behind her ears, were bad enough without having to contend with a totally manic mother. Here she was, five days away from her fourteenth birthday, with lopsided boobs, a wardrobe full of clothes that everyone had seen a thousand times and the absolute certainty of getting a C-minus for her geography project, and she hadn't even got a normal mother to turn to in her hour of need.

Normal mothers took you shopping and said things like, 'You choose – I'll pay.' Holly's mother considered clothes as merely a way of preventing hypothermia. She also seemed unable to grasp the

1

fact that Holly simply had to have some hipsters and a new pair of black boots and even less able to appreciate that if Holly was ever going to get Scott Hamill back from the clutches of Ella Hankinson, her wardrobe needed some serious updating.

Normal mothers came into your room in the mornings with a cup of tea and perched on the end of your bed and asked how your life was. Holly's mother, who had spent all Saturday taking a coachload of mums and toddlers to Clacton and most of Sunday slapping paint on the walls of the crèche at the Lowdown Centre, was so caught up with sorting out other people's lives that she barely realized Holly had one, let alone found time to ask how it was progressing.

Holly grabbed her blue-and-white bathrobe and padded across the landing to the bathroom, thinking that it was grossly unfair that a woman who gained enormous satisfaction from forcing the parishioners of St Saviour's into attending strawberry teas in aid of the crumbling bell tower, seemed totally devoid of any desire to deal with the crumbling social life of her *only* daughter.

This morning had been a case in point, she thought, peering in the mirror and scrutinizing her ivory skin for any sign of a spot. Ten minutes earlier, her mother, dressed in an ancient, shapeless cord skirt and a sage-green jumper of uncertain age, had flung open Holly's door and crashed into the bottom of her bed, thereby rudely wakening her from a most satisfying dream featuring her, Scott Hamill in his rugby gear and a very romantic stretch of tropical seashore.

'Marker pens, sweetheart!' her mother had cried.

Before Holly had managed to prise open one reluctant eyelid, her mother had been rummaging through her drawers like a thing possessed.

'Mum!' Holly had protested as her mother tossed make-up brushes and pots of lip-gloss on to the bed. 'What *are* you doing?'

'Looking for your coloured markers,' she had repeated, slamming one drawer shut and wrenching open another. 'Half of mine have dried out and I'm in a tearing hurry.'

'*Good morning, Holly darling, and how did you sleep?*' Holly had muttered sarcastically, sitting up in bed.

'What? Oh yes, sorry, sweetheart – sleep well?' her mother had responded distractedly, brushing a strand of greying hair from her eyes.

'Actually no,' admitted Holly. 'You see, I –'

'That's nice,' said her mother. 'Darling, where *are* those pens?'

Holly had sighed and raised her pewter-grey eyes heavenwards.

'In my school bag – what do you want them for anyway?'

'Posters, darling,' her mother had explained

3

enthusiastically, casting an eye around the assorted debris littering Holly's pale-blue carpet in an attempt to locate the school bag.

'Oh yes?' said Holly. 'And what is it this time? Hands off our Hostel? No Superstore for Swan's Meadow?' she chanted, listing her mother's two most recent projects. 'Of course', she added coaxingly, 'it could be that you are going to do a Come To Holly's Amazing Birthday Party poster.'

She waited, more in hope than expectation.

'Here they are!' cried her mother triumphantly, totally ignoring Holly's pointed hint and pulling a packet of felt markers from the top of her daughter's kitbag. 'I'm doing a couple of posters for the nursery raffle.'

And she headed for the door.

'Mum!' Holly had begun. Her mother had paused, hand on the doorknob, and eyed her daughter impatiently.

'What?'

'I need to talk to you,' Holly had begun.

Her mother had looked as astonished as if Holly had expressed a desire for them to go scuba-diving before breakfast.

'Darling, I've hardly time to breathe, never mind talk,' she gabbled. 'I've got these posters to drop off, and a committee meeting about the Michaelmas Fair and I haven't even looked at the agenda yet. Can't it wait?'

Holly shook her head adamantly.

'No, it's about Saturday,' she began, thinking that surely even her mother could see that Holly's birthday took precedence over discussions about bric-a-brac stalls.

Her mother clicked her tongue impatiently.

'Saturday? But that's days away!' she said. 'At the rate I'm going, it will be a miracle if I am still upright by Saturday.'

She caught Holly's miffed expression and softened.

'Look, if it's anything important, darling, we'll talk about it tonight,' she promised. 'Truly really.'

She glanced at her watch.

'Now I really must get on and so must you.'

'But, Mum . . .'

It was too late. Her mother had shut the door and pounded down the stairs muttering, 'Tickets twenty-five pence each or five for one pound.'

That's typical of my mother, Holly thought now, standing under the trickle of tepid water that passed for a shower in their ancient bathroom, and eyeing her non-developing boob anxiously. If it's anything important, indeed! She had forgotten. She knew she had. She could remember posters for some poxy raffle, but her daughter's birthday meant nothing to her at all.

Sometimes, thought Holly crossly, I wonder whether *I* mean anything at all.

While Holly was busy considering her mother's shortcomings, around the corner on Cattle Hill, Tansy Meadows was attempting to discipline her badly behaved hair and thinking about her father. This exercise was complicated somewhat by the fact that she hadn't a clue who he was. Her mother, on whom Tansy had pressed the issue several times, admitted that she wasn't oversure either, although she thought she could narrow it down to a choice of two.

Tansy adored her mother and was well used to her tendency to vagueness, but lately this gap in her ancestry had been bothering her more and more. All her friends at West Green Upper School had fathers somewhere or other; even Jade Williams had a dead one and lots of photographs in silver frames which people looked at and exclaimed, 'My, aren't you like your dad!'

Tansy assumed that she too must resemble her unknown father. Certainly she didn't bear any likeness whatsoever to her mother. Tansy was small and wiry with sandy-coloured flyaway hair, eyes the colour of snail shells and a fiercely determined nature. Her mother, Clarity (who had been christened Kathleen but who changed her name when she got in with a group of New Age travellers at the age of seventeen, because she thought it made her sound ethereal), was solidly built with a mass of frizzy auburn curls, hazel eyes and a temperament so laid back as to be almost horizontal. She drifted through life expecting everything and everyone to turn out just fine. Had she been a bit more switched on, Tansy thought, she might just have managed to keep closer tabs on the parentage of her child.

'Tansy! Breakfast's ready!' Her mother's voice called up the stairwell.

'Coming,' Tansy called back, abandoning her attempts to make her hair look sleek and sophisticated. She wondered what her mother's idea of breakfast would be today. Clarity Meadows may well have forsaken the open road and returned to more a more traditional lifestyle, but she still harboured pretty strong ideas about treating one's body as a temple. From time to time this led her to experiment with the most extraordinary diets and serve up platefuls of things that would have been much better left growing in a stretch of undisturbed woodland. It was supposed to be kids who had unconventional ideas, thought Tansy, clattering down the uncarpeted stairs and bashing her head against the wooden wind chimes which her mother insisted drew serenity into their living space. It seemed slightly unfair that when she only had one parent, she got landed with an eccentric one.

Tansy eyed the untidy sitting room with distaste.

The floral covers on the two battered armchairs were faded and frayed. Three large wrought iron candlesticks stood in one corner and a fat china Buddha grinned cheerfully from the fireplace. Piles of gardening magazines were stacked in every corner, whilst the coffee table was covered with seed catalogues and garden implements. Her mother referred to herself as a garden-design consultant. She spent most evenings drawing elaborate plans of patios and lily ponds, but her working day was spent mowing lawns, weeding borders and pruning rose bushes. Clarity loved her job because she said she could commune with nature all day. Unfortunately she didn't earn a great deal and while she repeatedly assured Tansy that money didn't buy you happiness, Tansy felt that it would be nice to have the opportunity of putting that theory to the test. Then they could have a big house with rag-rolled walls, thick carpets and a whirlpool bath. And her mother could get rid of her ancient and rusting van, which she insisted was ideal for her job, and the ownership of which Tansy said was so lacking in street cred as to be a punishable offence. She was sure her father, wherever he was, would not be driving such a disreputable vehicle.

Whenever she fantasized about her unknown father she imagined him as being well off, with a shock of sandy-coloured hair just like hers and a warm, all-encompassing smile. His shoes would be real leather and he would have a cashmere over-coat and a real pigskin wallet. Tansy liked beautiful things. And one day, whatever it took, she vowed she would have them.

'You're looking very thoughtful this morning,' remarked her mother, kissing the top of Tansy's head and dumping a bowl of something utterly extraordinary on to the wobbly Formica-topped table in the kitchen.

'I was thinking about my father,' said Tansy, peering suspiciously at the contents, 'whoever he might be.'

'Oh, that again,' sighed her mother. 'Darling, I've told you all I know.'

Tansy had, of course, on frequent occasions quizzed her mother about the two possible candidates for the role of father. One apparently was called Jordan and had spent a whole summer painting pebbles in a converted bus parked outside Glastonbury, before upping and leaving with a girl called October for a new life in the Faeroe Islands. The other had been called Pongo, which unfortunately for the detective in Tansy was not his real name, and he was an American university student from Illinois with whom her mother had had a brief fling in an attempt to get over the defection of the said Jordan. On balance, Tansy thought Pongo sounded more promising, apart from the unfortunate name. After all, if he had a degree he could be a successful business tycoon by now, or a TV personality or a wealthy lawyer with a big house and who took holidays in Florida. That he could also be out of work, penniless or a total jerk, Tansy refused to consider. She had great ambitions for her future, and if she couldn't have a father on hand to help her achieve them, she could at least dream about one who had achieved a few of the things to which she so earnestly aspired.

'Yes, that again,' retorted Tansy. 'Mum, you must know more than you've told me. I mean, you don't go having babies with people and not know something about them. At least, you shouldn't,' she added sharply.

Her mother sighed.

'You're right, sweetheart, of course you are,' she said. 'I was young, homesick, romantic, and very, very stupid. And in those days I wasn't a very good judge of men.'

Nothing's changed, thought Tansy. Her mother's latest boyfriend, Laurence Murrin, was a complete dork – a walking fashion disaster who considered himself to be a world authority on everything and could bore for England.

Clarity touched Tansy's shoulder.

'I'm sorry that you don't know your dad,' she whispered. 'I know it hasn't been easy for you – but it hasn't been a bed of roses for me either, you know.'

Tansy chewed her lip.

'Do you ever wish you hadn't gone ahead and had me?' she asked, scanning her mother's features.

'Darling, never!' cried her mother, hugging her close. 'I wouldn't be without you for the whole world.'

Tansy suddenly felt a great upsurge of love for her mum.

'I wouldn't be without you either,' she said. 'And anyway, who needs fathers?'

But still, one, somewhere, would be nice, she thought to herself, peering into her cereal bowl.

'What on earth is this?' she asked.

'It's a mixture of hazelnuts and wheatgerm and dried figs,' Charity said. 'I mixed it all up and added some wheat bran and then –'

'It's disgusting!' said Tansy, wrinkling her nose.

'Darling, it's brain food – I read up about it,' insisted her mother. 'Helps you concentrate. And now you're in Year Nine with all this new coursework, I thought . . .'

Clarity, who had spent most of her schooldays avoiding work, never failed to be amazed by her daughter's appetite for learning and information.

'Mum, it's no big deal – the work's easy.'

Tansy had found the first week of the new school year a doddle work-wise but something of a disappointment as far as romance was concerned. It wasn't that guys didn't ask her out, but she simply couldn't get excited over any of them. They were all so . . . ordinary. She wanted someone who was a total dish, with a wicked sense of humour, a functioning brain and loads of ambition, and that was a combination that was pretty thin on the ground at West Green Upper.

Just as Tansy was wondering if she could bring herself to swallow even one mouthful of her mother's idea of cereal, the telephone rang.

'Dunchester five-seven-seven-zero-seven-eight, Clarity Meadows speaking,' said her mother in her gardening-consultant-with-good-references voice.

'Oh, it's you, Cleo. Yes, yes, she's here – I'll hand you over.' She covered the mouthpiece and handed the receiver to Tansy.

'Cleo,' she said, 'sounding peeved. I'll go and try to persuade the van to start. And,' she added, gesturing to the bowl, 'eat.' Grabbing the car keys from a hook above the boiler, she kicked open the back door and disappeared.

'Hi, Cleo,' said Tansy, tipping the offending mixture into the pedal bin and grabbing a mango yoghurt from the fridge. 'You are an angel. You have just saved me from the breakfast from hell.'

7.50 a.m. 6 Kestrel Close, West Green, Dunchester. Otherwise known as Chaos City
'You don't know you're born,' Cleo told Tansy,

12

switching the receiver into her left hand and ramming a finger into her right ear in an attempt to block out the shouts emanating from behind the closed kitchen door. 'You should try living here for a day.'

How, she wondered, could breakfast, or any other time for that matter, be hell when there's just you and your mum living together in peaceful harmony? Right now Portia, her sixteen-year-old sister, was having a blazing row with her mum in the kitchen, Lettie, who was ten going on four, was sitting on the stairs, head in hands, doing the dramatic sobbing bit and saying she couldn't go to school because everyone was horrid to her, while Peaseblossom the cat, yet another member of the family who had failed to escape Mrs Greenway's passion for Shakespeare, was doing something exceedingly unsavoury on the doormat with the remains of a small butterfly.

'You have to help me,' pleaded Cleo down the phone to Tansy, while peering at herself in the hall mirror and wishing she had stunning cheekbones and a sylphlike figure. 'I haven't done any of my Geography homework and last term old Beetle said that if I handed in a single piece of work late this year, he would write to the parents. And that's all I need.'

'OK,' said Tansy cheerfully. 'You can look at mine when we get to school.'

13

'And your French?' asked Cleo tentatively, fiddling with a strand of crinkly blonde hair.

'Sure,' said Tansy, who always put work first as part of her campaign to become Somebody but who never minded sharing her endeavours with her friends. 'Er, what mega-brill things were you doing this weekend that stopped you working?'

Cleo swallowed. She didn't want to admit that her mum and stepdad had had another row or Portia had stormed out and gone walkabout and Lettie had thrown up because Lettie always threw up in a crisis. She didn't want to let on that it had been left to her to cook lunch and make her mum some camomile tea and persuade Roy, her stepdad, to come in from the garden shed, or that her precious Sunday afternoon had been spent taking Lettie for a walk while her mother and Roy attempted to become mature adults again. She didn't want to admit to Tansy that after it was all over, her mum had spent ages cuddling Lettie and saying she was sorry and everything would be fine now, and Roy had sat down with Portia and spent ages helping her with her German coursework and all they had said to Cleo was that she was the sensible one and what a good thing she never lost her head. And most of all she didn't want all her friends to know just how often these rows happened. It was bad enough that her mum and real dad had got divorced, without people knowing that the whole horrid arguing and fighting bit was beginning over again between her mother and Roy.

'Oh, we had visitors and stuff,' she said airily.

'Who?' asked Tansy, whose experience of visitors was that you usually wanted to use homework as an excuse to escape the boring chat. 'Was it a boy?'

Tansy knew that given the choice between equations and a decent guy, Cleo would forsake the maths in an instant.

'No it wasn't!' exclaimed Cleo. 'But talking of boys – guess who I saw on Saturday?'

'Who?' asked Tansy, spooning the last of the yoghurt into her mouth.

'Scott.'

'Holly's Scott?' queried Tansy.

'He's not Holly's Scott any more – he dumped her for Ella Hankinson, remember?'

'I know that,' said Tansy between bites of banana. 'But she reckons she can get him back. She's decided to throw this amazing party for her birthday and invite Scott and really lay it on. Ella's going to her grandparents' Ruby Wedding party in Norwich this weekend so she'll be out of the picture.'

'I don't actually think Ella is the only problem,' ventured Cleo. 'Oh, go away, Lettie,' she hissed as her sister tugged at her arm.

'What do you mean?' asked Tansy.

'I saw him on Saturday in Beckets Park.' She paused for effect.

'Yes?' urged Tansy

'With Jade. And they weren't just admiring the view.'

'Jade? Jade Williams? With Scott?' gasped Tansy. 'I don't believe it.'

Jade never seemed remotely interested in guys. Or in anything else really. Of course, she had had a terrible time. But still. Jade with Scott.

'Got to go – Mum's about to leave,' sighed Tansy down the phone. 'I'll meet you at the gate and you can tell me everything.'

'OK, and whatever you do don't say anything to Holly,' urged Cleo.

'Course I won't,' said Tansy. 'What's that noise?' she added.

'Oh sugar!' sighed Cleo. 'Lettie's thrown up on the cat.'

8.15 a.m. The Cedars. Feeling somewhat unwanted
Perhaps, thought Holly, ramming the geography homework that she hadn't done into her school bag and grabbing her hairbrush, my mother should never have had me.

Holly loved her mother dearly but she sometimes wondered whether she had been put out by the arrival of a daughter ten years after the birth of her second son. She knew that her conception had been something of a surprise to her parents. Her brothers, Thomas and Richard, were already ten and eleven when she arrived and her mother had decided to celebrate her imminent freedom from full-time child rearing by standing as prospective Labour candidate for Dunchester West. At a somewhat exclusive cheese and wine evening at Party headquarters, she had been smitten with a severe attack of nausea, which at the time she attributed to the rather dubious Wensleydale, but which turned out to be the beginnings of Holly.

Although Angela Vine had not been exactly overjoyed when Dr Penwithen beamed at her over his rimless spectacles and informed her, just four days after her fortieth birthday, that now there would be another little branch on the family Vine, she had rallied to the challenge with her normal fortitude, turning her attention from national politics to local issues, with the result that much of Holly's infancy was spent sleeping somewhat lopsidedly in a baby sling while her mother dished out chicken noodle soup at the local night shelter.

As Holly grew, and Mrs Vine decided that the playgrounds weren't safe enough, and that holiday playschemes weren't long enough, she began taking up the cause of the young. Or, as Holly was prone to mutter to anyone who would listen, other people's young. For as long as she could remember

Holly's parents had introduced her to their friends as 'Holly, our little afterthought' which made her feel like a PS at the end of a thank-you letter.

She brushed the tangles out of her shoulder-length hair and pounded downstairs to tackle her mother once again. But when she crashed through the kitchen door, nearly tripping over Naseby, her father's lilac Burmese cat who was playing the role of draught excluder, she found the paternal parent sitting at the table in his scarlet bathrobe, grey hair all awry, reading a copy of *History Today*. Of her mother there was no sign.

'She's gone to sort out a problem at the crèche,' said her father by way of explanation. 'She said to say goodbye.'

'Oh terrific,' muttered Holly flicking a strand of hair out of her eyes. '*Have a nice day, Holly; make a list for your birthday, Holly; decide how you want to celebrate, Holly.* Maybe if I was two years old with hammer toes and a glue-sniffing father, she'd notice my existence.'

'She enjoys it, dear,' he said benignly, peering at her over the top of his reading glasses. 'Women need to express themselves in the wider community.'

It would be nice, thought Holly, if she would give me time to express myself in the narrower one.

'Dad,' she began. 'Can I have a word? It's about Saturday.'

'Just a minute, dear,' he said, holding up his hand. 'I just want to finish this article. Absolutely fascinating – "Cromwell – Saint or Sinner?" Written by Doctor Entwhistle – you remember, he came for supper.'

Holly grunted non-committally and slotted two slices of bread into the toaster. So many strange people drifted in and out of their house that Holly tended to ignore all the ones that weren't male and under the age of twenty. Her father, Rupert, was a historian who spent his days closeted in his study at the top of the house writing biographies of long-dead generals. When he wasn't writing, he lectured on the Civil War at a variety of universities and colleges and held forth at great length on late-night radio programmes, all of which was just about bearable; and by way of relaxation, he dressed up as a Roundhead and fought mock battles with the Sealed Knot Society, which most definitely was not. The year before, he had appeared at the local carnival wearing an authentic but totally ridiculous-looking helmet and waving a pikestaff with unrestrained enthusiasm. Nick Balfour, who was the loudmouth of Year Eight, had seen him and told all his mates that Holly's father was a loop. She had wanted to lie down somewhere very dark and quietly die. Having a

manic mother was bad enough but being lum-
bered with a sixty-year-old father who still played
soldiers was more than any human being should be
expected to bear.

Holly turned on the tap over the sink to fill the
kettle. There were several loud clunks and the
merest trickle of sandy-coloured water.

'Dad, the pipes are playing up again,' sighed
Holly.

'What's that, dear?' murmured her father, not
raising his eyes from the magazine.

'The pipes,' repeated Holly. 'Dad, you'll have to
get the plumber. Mum will go spare.'

The other passion in Rupert Vine's life was the
house. The Cedars. It was also a source of great
disagreement between Holly's parents. Her mother
wanted to move to a modern house with windows
that fitted and radiators that didn't clank and
ceilings that you could reach without first finding
a three-metre ladder. Her father, who vastly pre-
ferred the past to the present, refused point blank to
even consider the matter, saying that modern
houses had no soul and that Vines had lived at The
Cedars for over a hundred years which accounted
for the sense of continuity and history which pervaded the place. To which Holly's mother replied
that as far as she could see all that pervaded the
place was a whole lot of dust, some rising damp and
the occasional adventurous mouse.

Their house had been built by Holly's great-grandfather, Ambrose, who had loads of money. It had been handed down through the generations to Holly's dad, who didn't. Which was why three months earlier, after some very strongly worded letters from the bank, her dad had sold off most of the rambling back garden to a builder who assured him that the site would be perfect for a couple of executive homes of taste and discretion. Now there were earthmovers where the orchard used to be, with two almost finished houses on the far side of the newly erected back fence, and all the water was a sallow shade of orange.

Holly had been really cheesed off when the bull-dozers moved in, but Cleo told her to look on the positive side.

'Just think,' she had said one day as they sat under the one remaining tree looking at the boy posters in *Sugar* magazine, 'your destiny could lie in one of those houses.'

Holly had stared at her quizzically.

'Well,' Cleo had explained, 'for all you know some gorgeous guy might move in, catch sight of you and fall irretrievably in love with you. Then all your problems would be solved.'

Cleo was very keen on happy endings. She also knew how desperately Holly wanted to fall in love.

Holly's love life was an even greater worry to her than her mother's unreasonable behaviour or her

21

disappointing figure. The awful truth was that she had only ever had one boyfriend. She'd been out with Scott Hamill for three weeks and two days, and stood on the touchline while he played rugby and cheered in all the right places, only to lose him to Ella Hankinson, who had baby blonde hair and a thrusting chest. Holly was sure it was the chest that had clinched it. She had pretended not to care. But she did. Dreadfully.

She buttered her toast, convinced there was something wrong with her; no one normal got to the age of fourteen without ever having been properly kissed. Scott had given her a couple of quick pecks on the lips but there had been nothing long and lingering and it was proving very difficult to take an active part in the lunch-hour discussions on passion when you had never experienced it at first hand.

Perhaps it was because she was tall. She had tried sagging at the knees when she thought Scott wanted to kiss her, but it got very uncomfortable waiting for it to happen. If only she was tiny like Tansy, she would probably be kissed to distraction.

Her only good points, she thought sadly, were her ivory skin and a decent-shaped mouth, but that was about it. In addition to the lopsided boobs, which meant wearing baggy sweaters and thinking up endless excuses to get out of swimming, she had thick ebony eyebrows which, unless she disciplined

22

them regularly with tweezers, threatened to meet over her nose. Tansy said strong eyebrows were a sign of a deeply sensual and passionate nature. Holly said it would be nice to have the opportunity to put her dormant sensuality to the test. Preferably on the errant Scott.

And her birthday had to be it. If she could just get her mother to agree to a proper party, the works, the real biz, she was sure she would have a chance of getting him back. If only she could make the most of Ella's absence by getting Scott in a darkened room with some suitable smoochy music and the chat-up lines she had memorized from last month's *It's Bliss!*, she could crack it, she knew she could.

'Well, I'd better take this upstairs and get started,' said her father, getting slowly to his feet. He was almost sixty and always joked that his knees were seventy-five.

'Dad,' said Holly quickly, deciding that in the absence of her mother she might at least try her tactics on her paternal parent. 'About Saturday . . .'

'Saturday?' Her father peered at her enquiringly. 'Oh yes, Saturday.' His face brightened. 'Big day. Looking forward to it.'

Holly's heart leapt. So they hadn't forgotten. Brilliant.

Go for it, Holly. Now.

'Can I invite loads of friends?' she added quickly.

'Friends?' For someone who had won the Hubbard Prize for Historical Biography he could be amazingly slow on the uptake.

'On Saturday,' Holly urged.

'Well, I suppose so, but . . .' Her father rubbed his stubbly chin and looked doubtful.

'We won't be any trouble,' she added earnestly. 'Please, Dad.'

'Well, yes, of course, if you really want to,' said her father, frowning slightly. 'But I thought –'

'Oh, great, Dad, thanks a million.' She flung her arms round his neck, a gesture which caused him to look even more astonished.

'Must dash,' she said, stuffing the remains of her toast into her mouth. 'I can't wait to tell the others.'

Her father watched as she tore into the hall, grabbed her school bag and shot out of the front door, and shook his head in bewilderment.

The dear child really was full of surprises. It must be with her being a girl.

8.30 a.m. Class 9C, West Green Upper School
Jade Williams dumped her kitbag on the classroom floor and sat down. She was glad no one else had arrived yet. Getting to school early was the one way of getting time out for herself. Being alone was a total impossibility at home.

Not that she could get into the way of thinking

24

of her aunt's house as home. Home had been the little Regency house in Brighton, so close to the sea that you could hear the waves breaking on the shingle. Home had been her attic bedroom with the sloping ceiling and wonky floorboards. At home no one teased her about being thirteen and still having fluffy pandas and rabbits and a giant kangaroo at the foot of her bed. Home had been friendly and comfortable. Home had been Mum and Dad.

Jade felt the inevitable tears pricking at the back of her eyes again and gave herself a shake. There was no Mum and Dad any more. There hadn't been since that awful Tuesday evening back in May when they had driven off in their clapped-out old Escort, waving and laughing, to celebrate their wedding anniversary with dinner at *Mon Plaisir* in Worthing.

'Now don't go spending all evening on the phone and do your homework and don't leave lights on all over the place,' her mother had said. 'Oh dear, I do wish we'd asked Karen to come over and sit with you – I hate leaving you here on your own.'

'Oh, Mum, for heaven's sake,' Jade had snapped. 'I'm not some stupid kid. I don't need looking after.'

'Oh, and Jade,' her mother had added, as her husband elbowed her towards the door, 'you could try and tidy your room. It is a tip.'

'Nag, nag, nag,' said Jade pulling a face.

She wished she hadn't.

Her dad had given her a hug.

'See you later, Sunshine,' he had grinned, giving her a friendly punch on the shoulder.

But she hadn't seen them later. She had never seen them again. On the way back from the restaurant, a joyrider driving a stolen BMW had crossed the central reservation on the new bypass and crashed into her parents' car. The police-woman told her that her mum had died instantly. Her father died in the ambulance on the way to hospital.

Jade blocked out the rest the way she always did. She refused to think about the funeral, about the family discussions on 'what to do with Jade'. She wouldn't let herself think about the 'For Sale' board being hammered into the pocket-sized lawn or her mum's clothes being bundled up in plastic bags by her gran and taken to a charity shop.

She missed her parents so much. And she missed Tanya, who had been her best friend since primary school. On the day that her mum's sister, Paula, had driven down with her husband, David, to fetch her and bring her to Dunchester, Tanya had come to say goodbye. Jade had cried and cried. She had hugged Tanya and they had promised one another that they would write and phone and visit, but next to hearing the news about Mum and Dad, driving away and leaving Tanya waving frantically was the worst feeling in the whole world. Paula and David had kids of their own and Jade felt as if there was no one left who was just for her.

'Don't worry, cherub,' Paula had said comfortingly. 'You'll make lots of friends at your new school. And just think, you've got Allegra for a buddy now.'

Jade started unpacking her school bag and sighed as she thought about her three cousins. She could just about handle Joshua, who was sixteen and a total dweeb who kept out of her way most of the time, and Nell, who was seven and quite cute when she wasn't picking her nose and sticking snot on the skirting boards, but Allegra was something else. She was fourteen and a half – a year older than Jade – and went to a stage school on the other side of town. She was stunningly beautiful – and didn't she know it! Her dressing table was covered with lotions and creams and almost every shade of eye colour ever manufactured and her wardrobe was full of the funkiest gear you could imagine. She had stacks of CDs which she played all the time, refusing to let Jade play any of her own, which she said were totally sad.

The worst thing of all was that in front of her parents, Allegra was all sweetness and light, saying how lovely it was to have Jade around, and of course she would be nice to her, poor little thing, and would she like to borrow her chenille sweater. But as soon as they were on their own, she turned really bitchy and catty, saying that Jade's clothes were more suited to an unimaginative nine-year-old than a teenager and rummaging through her make-up basket saying things like, 'Oh, puhleese!' and 'That colour went out three seasons ago.'

Ever since Jade first moved in, she and Allegra had had to share a bedroom which was something Jade just couldn't get used to.

'It will do you good to have someone with you to take your mind off things, cherub,' Paula had explained, as if talking about blusher and boys would make Jade forget her mum and dad. In fact, Paula didn't seem to want Jade to talk about the past at all. If she found Jade crying, she would jolly her along and offer her a game of Outburst! or a trip to the cinema. She even suggested that Jade should put away her collection of family photographs because they might be upsetting her – but Jade flatly refused. She loved to look at them; to see bits of her mum and dad in herself. She had her mum's mass of honey-coloured hair which tumbled untidily over her head, and her father's piercing green eyes. The last thing she did at night and the very first thing she did in the morning was talk to the photos of Mum and Dad. Silently, inside her head, so that Allegra wouldn't tease her.

Assorted kids were beginning to drift in to the classroom. Some of them smiled briefly at Jade and said a quick, 'Hi!' but most of them ignored her. It was pretty hard starting a new school mid-year and besides, it seemed that once the other kids knew that her parents had been killed, they got embarrassed and didn't know what to say. Jade knew they weren't being mean – it was more that they were scared about saying the wrong thing; she just wished they'd say something – anything to make her feel part of things again.

'What if no one likes me?' she had ventured apprehensively one evening when Paula was showing her the school prospectus.

'Of course they will like you,' she insisted. 'Just don't be – well, you know . . . don't dwell on the past.'

'And just think,' David had added, trying to lighten things, 'with looks like yours, you'll have all the boys in Year Nine falling over themselves to ask you out.'

To date, thought Jade, she hadn't exactly been trampled in the rush. Not that it mattered. She was so busy trying to keep cheerful and not burst into tears that flirting and chatting up boys would just be too much of an effort. Although, Scott Hamill was nice. After that horrendously embarrassing moment in the park the previous weekend, he'd been so – well, so ordinary about it. Most guys she had known in the past would have run a mile. But he was different. If she was going to try to get off with anyone, it would be him.

'Hi, Jade!' Holly Vine hurtled into the classroom. 'Hey, what's up – you look like you've been crying.'

Holly was always one to come straight to the point with her friends even if she rarely managed it with her parents.

'I'm fine,' muttered Jade, wishing her freckled nose didn't go red whenever she cried.

'Is it because of your parents?' asked Holly gently. 'It must be awful – I don't blame you for feeling mizz.'

Jade looked at her gratefully. Holly had been the first person to talk to her when she came to West Green Upper last term, and the only one not to pretend her mum and dad had never existed. Because of Holly, she was getting to know Tansy and Cleo as well – but like everyone else, they never mentioned Mum and Dad.

'It's four months today that it happened,' she whispered, scrabbling in her school bag and pulling out her geography folder.

Holly bit her lip. She didn't really know what to say.

'That's hard,' she murmured and then thought how inadequate that sounded. 'Well, anyway,' she said cheerfully, thinking that perhaps Jade needed to talk about something else, 'it's on. It's all systems go.'

'Pardon?' asked Jade.

'The party – I told you,' insisted Holly, incredulous that anyone could forget this forthcoming highlight of Year Nine's social calendar. 'My dad came up with the goods and said I could have it.'

'That's nice,' said Jade unenthusiastically. The last thing she felt like right now was a party with everyone being hip and happening and her feeling the pits.

'And you can sleep over,' said Holly. 'I'm getting my best mates to stay on after so we can have a post-mortem on who got off with who!'

Holly, who sounded quite scatty to people who didn't know her frightfully well but who was really pretty astute about other people's feelings, knew that the sleeping over bit could be the key to getting Jade to come.

As Holly expected, Jade perked up a bit.

'Who's going?' she asked. Holly thought she was one of her best mates. That was really nice.

'Well, Tansy and Cleo and you and me, and then I'm asking Tim and Becky and Alex Gregson and Nick – which means asking Ursula, of course, 'cos they're tied at the hip – and Scott . . .' she added, trying to look totally casual as she mentioned his name.

Scott, thought Jade.

'And Ella?' she asked.

Holly shook her head.

'She's away at some family bash,' she said, trying to make the whole issue sound totally unimportant. 'So you will come, won't you? It'll be a blast.'

Jade thought. It seemed all wrong to think about parties with her mum and dad dead. Like laughing in church or playing tag round gravestones in the churchyard. And she didn't have anything to wear. But then again, she had to get to know people. And it would mean a whole night away from Allegra, which had to be a bonus. And Scott was going to be there.

'OK,' she said, 'that would be good.'

'Ace!' beamed Holly. 'I'm going to make next Saturday a day that no one will ever forget!'

12.30 p.m. The cafeteria

Holly hurtled into the cafeteria, grabbed a table in the corner and scanned the crowded room for her friends. She had had no chance of talking to them all morning. Tansy was clever enough to be in the top sets for almost everything, and while Holly had been grappling with the complexities of the German language, Cleo and Jade had been making filo pastry in Home Economics and tie-dying in CDT.

'Hey, you guys – over here!' Holly spotted

her friends struggling with laden trays and waved frantically.

'Guess what?' she enthused, after they had settled themselves down. 'It's on!'

'What's on?' asked Tansy, prising the lid off her plastic lunch box and eyeing a carrot and cottage cheese sandwich suspiciously.

'My party,' said Holly.

'Really?' Tansy looked impressed. 'That's great!'

Holly nodded.

'So your mum agreed after all?' asked Cleo, spooning the school's idea of macaroni cheese into her mouth at high speed.

'No, I asked Dad instead,' admitted Holly. 'And he said yes, just like that. And he said I could invite loads of people. And you guys can sleep over!'

Cleo paused in mid-chew. The party might be fun, but a sleepover? No way. She couldn't. She'd have to come up with an excuse.

'I can't wait!' enthused Holly. 'It'll be so cool.'

'What'll be cool?' A broad American accent broke in on their conversation. 'Hey, Scotty, let's sit here, why not?'

The four girls turned and gawped. Deftly balancing a tray on one hand and nudging Scott Hamill playfully with his free arm, was the most drop-dead gorgeous guy any of them had ever seen. He was wearing a black polo sweatshirt, joggers and a baseball cap. He grinned at them all.

That guy, thought Holly, taking in his slate-grey eyes and floppy blond hair, is seriously sexy.

That guy's sweatshirt, thought Tansy, who could smell money at twenty paces, is a Ralph Lauren and it's definitely not a fake. His body isn't bad either.

Isn't Scott dreamy? thought Jade.

'This is Trig Roscoe,' announced Scott, interrupting their thoughts and giving them the info they were all dying to know. 'He's going to be here for a year because his dad's got a transfer to Dunchester. Mr Roscoe is an ex-Marine.'

This latter piece of information obviously impressed Scott as much as Trig's looks were impressing the girls.

'Oh, and he's American,' added Scott unnecessarily.

'From Westmont, Illinois,' declared Trig, opening a packet of crisps with his teeth.

Illinois, thought Tansy with a jolt. That's where my perhaps-father came from.

'Near Chicago,' Trig added.

'Deep pan pizzas,' said Cleo, for whom food was a source of the greatest joy. 'And the Bulls.'

'Wow!' breathed Trig. 'An English kid who knows about basketball. How come?'

'I've got a sister with a sports-mad boyfriend and

a father who watches endless sport on Sky TV,' said Cleo ruefully.

Trig laughed and looked at her admiringly. Cleo was too busy demolishing an apple turnover to notice.

Tansy, who was fascinated by everything American, introduced everyone.

'Hi!' she said. 'I'm Tansy Meadows, and this is Holly Vine and Jade Williams and that's Cleo . . .'

Trig smiled at Cleo.

Just then Ella Hankinson simpered up and smiled coyly at Scott. Her school blouse was tucked tightly into her short skirt. When she sat down, she swung one leg gracefully over the other.

Holly bristled, conscious of Ella's perfectly symmetrical chest and sure she chose her blouses one size too small just in order to show it off.

'Hi, Scott – missed you,' Ella said. 'Hi, Trig! About this weekend, Scott . . .'

She continued but whispered in Scott's ear, so no one else could hear.

How pathetic, thought Holly. Trig, meanwhile, seemed to have problems adjusting to English life.

'Boy, this place is sure different from Westmont Junior High. Bizarre clothes, soggy French fries and no baseball on TV. Is everyone really sad or is there life in Dunchester?'

Oh please, thought Cleo. Attitude or what?

35

'Actually,' said Holly, 'there is. Or at least, there will be on Saturday.' She flicked a strand of hair over her left shoulder, a gesture which *Sugar* said was a real turn-on for most guys. 'On Saturday I am having the party to end all parties. Come along, why don't you?'

For a second, Trig looked doubtful.

'I dunno,' he said. 'My girlfriend – well, girl-friends – they're both back in the States and I don't know anyone yet.' He looked upwards in mock horror. 'Did they freak out when they heard I was coming to England!'

Bully for them, thought Holly. I bet they had chests too.

'You can come with Scott,' she said, who on hearing his name promptly turned round.

Yes! said Jade to herself, mentally going through her wardrobe.

'Are you going to be there?' Trig asked Cleo.

'Yes,' Cleo replied shortly. Although preferably as far away from you as possible, she thought.

'OK,' said Trig. 'Cool. I'll come.'

He said it as though he was granting a great favour. Tansy looked well satisfied.

'But *you* won't be going, will you, Scott?' purred Ella, her nose three centimetres from Scott's left eyeball. 'I'm going away, remember.'

Jade and Holly held their breath.

'I'll go anyway,' Scott replied casually. 'To keep

Trig company.' It sounded a good excuse, but Cleo noticed that he was smiling directly at Jade. She threw an anxious glance in Holly's direction but her friend appeared not to have noticed. Ella, meanwhile, was looking like thunder. If looks could have killed, thought Cleo, Holly and Scott would be en route for the mortuary. Her thoughts were interrupted by the end-of-lunch bell.

'I must go,' Cleo said, dumping her dirty dishes on the trolley. 'Choir practice. You coming, Jade?'

Everyone started to disperse.

'Me too,' agreed Tansy. 'Drama club.' Tansy was very theatrically inclined, something which her mother said tended to point the finger of fatherhood at Jordan, who could make a drama out of a crisis. Tansy chose to ignore this, having decided that Pongo was a far better bet than a guy who painted pebbles.

'Hey, you guys,' protested Holly, as they walked from the cafeteria across the school forecourt together. 'I wanted you to help me with ideas for the party. Food and music and all that stuff. There's loads to do.'

'Indeed there is, Holly Vine!' Mr Grubb, known to everyone as Beetle, appeared from the doorway of the Science Block. 'Much to do. Like explaining the absence of your geography project.'

Holly gulped. The others drifted off. You didn't hang around when Beetle was roused.

37

'Ah well, sir, you see, sir, actually what happened was that –'

'Shall we discuss this well-thought-out excuse inside?' he replied. 'Then I can ignore it, you can complain that I am horribly unfair and we can agree that tomorrow you will stay late for detention and write me an additional essay. Agreed?'

Now I won't be able to go shopping for gear after school, thought Holly. My whole life put on hold because of some stupid essay. Who cares about river valleys anyway?

TUESDAY

8 a.m. In the kitchen at The Cedars.
In acquisitive mode

HOLLY'S BIRTHDAY LIST
Red hipsters
Lemongrass shower gel
Mud face pack
Watch
Boots size 4
Compilation CDs
Personal CD player
Money – lots of it

STUFF FOR HOLLY'S PARTY
Loads of cola, lemonade, etc.
etc.
Crisps and nuts
Mini hot dogs
Pizzas – masses
That gooey chocolate cake
you make

'Mum, I've made these lists . . .' Holly dashed into the kitchen to find her mother talking in a most agitated manner on the telephone and her father spreading three inches of lime marmalade on to his wholemeal toast.

'Richard, darling, NO! Oh surely not? She did? You were? He has?' Her voice rose to a crescendo in competition with the earthmovers outside. 'But, Richard dear, of *course* you must – no trouble, no trouble at all. All right, talk to you later. Love you lots. Bye for now.'

She banged the receiver back on to the rest and turned to her husband. Holly opened her mouth to speak and shut it again when it became clear that neither parent was going to take the slightest notice.

'Rupert, would you believe it? Serena has walked out. Just like that. Upped and offed. Poor Richard, he's in pieces, bless him.'

Richard was Holly's twenty-five-year-old married brother. He was brilliant at being an accountant and terrible at changing nappies, which was a bit of a drawback since he had an eighteen-month-old son called William who was totally circular and utterly adorable, particularly when asleep.

'Rupert!' repeated Holly's mum. 'Serena's left Richard.'

'Has she?' said Holly's father, biting into his toast and marmalade and showing about as much surprise as if he had been informed that the sun had risen that morning. 'She'll go back. She always does.'

Richard and Serena had a relationship that at best was lively and at worst explosive. Holly was very fond of her brother but felt that there were rather more pressing matters to be attended to.

'Mum . . .' she tried again, one eye on the clock.

'I must go over there,' interrupted her mother. 'She's left William with him and he's teething.'

'William or Richard?' enquired Holly's father a mite sarcastically, getting up from the table and picking up his briefcase.

Her mother glared at him.

'Well,' he said, 'I must be off – I've to be in Oxford by ten and the traffic is bound to be frightful. And don't forget I'm staying over tonight – decent dinner in Hall with the Master. Serves a damn fine port if I recall.'

'But, Rupert, what about poor Richard?' insisted his wife.

'He doesn't like port as far as I know,' he replied, deliberately misunderstanding.

'Rupert!'

'Angela,' said Rupert firmly. 'What do you expect me to do? Richard is twenty-five, a married man and a father. He has to sort out his own problems. You fuss and worry over him as if he were Holly's age.'

And you don't fuss or worry over me at all, thought Holly irritably. After her father had gone she had another go.

'Mum, about Saturday – I've done lists. Dad said –'

'Lists?' Her mother looked surprised and took the sheets of paper from Holly's outstretched hand. She had just put on her reading glasses when the phone shrilled urgently once more.

'Richard? Oh he hasn't? All right. Don't worry – I'm on my way.'

She turned to Holly.

'Must dash, darling – William's stuffed rice krispies in his ear.'

'But, Mum, aren't you going to look at my lists?' protested Holly.

Her mother picked up the sheets of paper.

'I'll take them with me,' she said. 'I must say, it's nice that you're taking an interest. Now – want a lift as far as the roundabout?'

As Holly clambered into her mother's metallic-blue Metro she wondered why anyone wouldn't take an interest in their own birthday. Except of course that her mother wasn't a party person. And she was very middle-aged. And not at all socially switched on.

'I'll be a bit late home tonight,' said Holly as her mother pulled up at the kerbside. 'Netball practice.'

It didn't seem sensible to raise the matter of the detention. Her mother had a tendency to go ballistic over unfinished work and to do ridiculous things like grounding you or stopping your allowance. She didn't want to mention anything that would put this party at risk. Not with her dad being so co-operative and everything finally sorted.

She gave herself a little hug. By Saturday night she would have Scott back. She just knew she would.

10.45 a.m.
In Biology
Cleo folded the note ready to slip it to Tansy when the bell rang. She was getting a bit worried about Holly's party. For one thing she didn't have any decent gear to wear, and for another she was quite sure that while Holly would be flirting like crazy with Scott, and Tansy would have dozens of boys round her because Tansy always did, no one would chat her up. And she knew it was all because she was fat.

Dear Tansy,
I'm writing this in Biology and I'm bored! Who cares about cellular respiration?
What are you going to wear to Holly's party? What are you getting her? I reckon Jade is after Scott which is awful because Holly's desperate to get him back and Jade's supposed to be a friend. Should we warn Holly, do you think?
What did you think of Trig?
Pretty full of himself, I reckon.
Love, Cleo

Boys were perfectly friendly to her but they never got any further, not even when she took notice of all the tips given to her by her sister,

Tuesday

Portia, who knew all there was to know about the art of seduction on account of her ongoing romance with Gareth Perryman in Year Eleven.

'You're too uptight; you have to chill,' Portia instructed her. 'And don't look as if you care about anything – look unavailable. Boys always want what they think they can't have.'

Maybe, thought Cleo, shoving her biology folder into her bag as the bell rang, she should impart this information to Holly. Cleo was absolutely certain that Jade was after Scott and she knew full well that Holly wanted him back more than anything else in the world. The two of them had been friends ever since playgroup. Holly had always stuck up for her when people called her Fatty. Cleo really wanted Holly to be happy and if keeping Jade away from Scott would do the trick, then that's what she would have to spend the party doing. There was unlikely to be much else on offer.

11.30 a.m. In Physics

Dear Cleo,
Thanks for the note. I haven't got a single garment worth wearing, but I'm working on Mum. I fancy a suede miniskirt – what do you think?

I don't know that you are right about Jade – I reckon that because of her mum and dad she's not likely to be in the mood for pulling. And even if she did fancy him, she's too timid to try it on.

Why don't we club together and get Holly some smellies?
Love, Tansy.
PS Trig's OKish, I suppose.

Actually, thought Tansy, doodling a clown face at the end of her note, Trig is a lot more than OK. Trig is utterly swoon-inducing and to die for. It wasn't just his glorious eyes and that sensational smile, it was the whole confidence bit, the way he was totally at ease, completely sure of himself. OK, so he poked fun, but even that was a turn-on. Ever since yesterday at lunch, she had been unable to stop thinking about him, which was an unusual experience for her because although heaps of guys chatted her up, she frankly found most of them boring, immature and ordinary. And Tansy had no place for ordinary in her life.

There was, of course, the added bonus that Trig was American. And from Illinois. For all she knew, he might live in the same town as her unknown father. Half of her knew that this was about a zillion-to-one chance, but the other half was quite enjoying fantasizing about Trig falling madly in love with her, and inviting her to America when he went home, and them meeting Tansy's dad who would recognize her instantly and rush over with tears in his eyes and –

'Tansy Meadows!' Mrs Bainbridge interrupted her reverie. 'For the third time of asking, could you possibly rouse yourself enough to give us the answer to question nine?'

'Er . . .' murmured Tansy, trying to find her place.

45

Tuesday

'Or perhaps you would like to share with the rest of us whatever fascinating thought was occupying your mind when you should have been considering terminal velocity?' added Mrs Bainbridge sarcastically.

No, thought Tansy. I don't think so. I think that just for now, I shall play it really cool. If Cleo is right and Jade and Holly are both after Scott, and Cleo doesn't even like Trig, then it's up to me to make him feel at home.

Thinking about just how she might do that kept her occupied for the rest of the day.

3.30 p.m. During study period - not studying

Dear Tanya,

Thanks for your letter and the photograph. Your new hairstyle is brill – you look heaps older!

I need your advice. There's this guy in my year and he's really cute. I think he might like me but he's going out with this girl, Ella, who's got an amazing figure and is really flash. Anyway, Holly – that's the girl I told you about last term – is having a party on Saturday and Scott's going WITHOUT ELLA! What shall I wear? How do I play it? And do you think I'm awful to be thinking about boys after all that has happened?

It would be nice to have someone just for me. Miss you heaps.

Tons of love,

JADE

XXXXXXX

Jade licked the envelope and stuffed the letter in her bag to post on the way home. She could have phoned Tanya but if she did that, Allegra would hover in the hallway, eavesdropping on every word and mimicking her every expression, and no way was Jade going to admit to her cousin that she fancied a boy. She felt guilty enough about even thinking of having a good time with Mum and Dad dead, and besides, if she didn't admit her feelings to anyone she wouldn't feel a complete nerd if Scott totally ignored her.

As soon as the bell rang, she piled her books in her bag and ran downstairs to the girls' cloakroom. As she turned the corner to her locker, she bumped into Holly.

'Hi!' she said. 'Walk to the bus stop? I could do with some advice on what to wear for your party.'

Holly shook her head.

'Detention,' she said, pulling a face. 'But say, why don't you come on over tonight? You can help me try this new super-seductive makeover that's in *Sugar* magazine and we can sort out the music and stuff.'

'Great!' enthused Jade. 'But won't your mum mind me just turning up?'

'Course not,' said Holly emphatically. 'Chances are she'll be out at some committee meeting or other.'

*

47

5.15 p.m. After detention

'All right, hand in your work and you may all go.' Miss Partridge (who was taking detention) put the top on her pen and picked up her bag.

Holly slouched up to her desk and handed in the essay that Beetle had set her.

'Oh, Holly dear,' said Miss Partridge, who had a very soft spot for Holly because she was as brilliant at English as she was dire at Geography, 'will you thank your father so much for his note?'

'Miss?'

'About the battle re-enactment on Saturday,' she said. 'I shall be there – dressed up and ready to go as Worried Bystander.' She gave a peal of laughter. 'I'm so thrilled your father got me involved in the Sealed Knot – isn't it exciting?'

It was, thought Holly, amazing how some people got their thrills.

'Oh very,' she said. 'Can I go now?'

She grabbed her rucksack and charged downstairs. If she was lucky, she might meet up with Scott who had athletics practice on Tuesdays. She dashed through the double doors into the main corridor. Straight into Trig Roscoe. He was wearing a black tracksuit and trainers but still managed to look like a pin-up in *It's Bliss*.

'Hey, where's the fire?' he said.

'Oh, hi!' Holly gulped. 'Sorry.'

He grinned and Holly felt her cheeks burn.

'That's OK – can't wait to get out of the place, eh? Me neither.'

'Were you in detention too?' asked Holly, thinking it was unusual for a new guy to get punished that early no matter what they'd done.

Trig shook his head.

'Extra History – we don't do English History in the States.'

'Lucky you!' said Holly.

'I kind of like it,' said Trig. 'All your kings and barons and stuff – it's great. I'm really into all that.'

'My dad's a historian,' commented Holly. 'That, and sadly deranged on the side.'

'Really? You mean, he earns his living through history? Wow! I'd sure like to meet him.'

No way, thought Holly. He's best kept behind closed doors.

Trig glanced at his watch, which had as many dials on it as the flight deck of Concorde.

'Come on – I said I'd meet Scott at the bus stop.'

Scott. Holly's heart gave a little flutter.

Trig opened the outside door and stood back for her to go through. He grinned. Holly's heart decided to go into overdrive.

'So what gives on your party?' he said as they crossed the yard to the bus stop.

'How do you mean?' Holly asked, thinking what gorgeous eyes he had.

'Well – you know – what's the scene? Is it a

49

cookout or a rave? It's not a pool party, is it?' He looked slightly anxious.

Holly laughed.

'No way,' she said. 'We don't have swimming pools left, right and centre like you do in the States.'

Trig looked relieved. 'We have some great parties back in Illinois,' he said. 'My cousin had a swell Rock and Rodeo party last Fall. But then I suppose you uptight Brits never get to hang loose like that,' he teased.

Holly swallowed. She had been so ecstatic at getting her dad to agree to the party that she hadn't thought further than buying some cola and crisps and borrowing as many of her mates CDs as she could.

She was about to say that it was just an ordinary, run of the mill, dark room, loud music, parent-free-zone party when she stopped. For some reason she didn't want Trig to think she was in any way ordinary. Not that she fancied him or anything. Well, not much. But she wanted him to think her hip and happening and really at the cutting edge. (She wasn't sure what the cutting edge meant but she'd read somewhere that it was where you were meant to be.)

'Oh,' she said airily, in what she hoped was a husky and seductive voice, 'now that would be telling.'

'Go on, tell me,' he urged. 'Does Scott know?'

'Do I know what?' Scott loped up to the bus stop, still dressed in his white running shorts and singlet. I do love him, thought Holly, and I will get him back. I will, I will, I will.

And of course, if for any reason I don't, there is always Trig.

'Do you know the theme of Holly's party?' Trig repeated. 'She's not letting on.'

'Theme?' asked Scott in a bewildered voice. Most parties were just opportunities for dancing, chatting and, if you got lucky, a bit of serious kissing. 'Isn't it just an ordinary party?'

Holly shook her head.

'There will', she asserted, 'be nothing ordinary about it.'

6 p.m. Intent on sorting her mother
When Holly arrived home her mother was on the phone. She covered the mouthpiece with one hand, mouthed, 'It's Dad,' and carried on talking.

Holly went upstairs, tore off her uniform, put on her favourite jeans and her 'I'm So Cool' T-shirt and picked up a pad and pen. She hoped Jade wouldn't be long – and that she was hot on ideas. Now that she had hinted to Trig and Scott that this party was going to be something special she had to come up with something truly amazing.

She kicked off her shoes and lay on the bed. Trig

51

was gorgeous. She wondered what it would be like to be kissed by him. She closed her eyes and did a little puckering of the lips. Then again, she really loved Scott big time. She imagined him running his hands down her back. She was just getting to the shivery tingly bit when she remembered that she hadn't got her mum sorted yet.

As she ran downstairs, she heard her mother raise her voice.

'I said, I really ought to get something good to wear for Saturday – can't let the side down! Well, of course it's important. Well, it is to me anyway.'

Oh no, thought Holly. She doesn't actually think she is going to *appear* at my party, does she? Everyone knows parents go out or at the very least sit upstairs in their bedrooms with the TV and sandwiches. They certainly do not hang around in their idea of high fashion making spectacles of themselves. She walked into the kitchen just as her mother hung up.

'Er, Mum,' said Holly, 'you're not going to actually be *at* my party on Saturday, are you? I mean, while it's actually going on?'

Her mother walked purposefully to the fridge and took out a packet of sausages. She was not a mother who worried about low-fat diets.

'No, Holly dear, I am not,' she said, peeling off the cling film.

Thank heavens for that, thought Holly.

'Because I'm afraid you've got a little carried away with all this,' she continued, piercing the sausages with a skewer. 'There is absolutely no way you can have a party on Saturday night.'

Holly's stomach suddenly felt as if it had been filled with lead. No party? There had to be a party. She had told everyone there was going to be a party. Even Dad had agreed that there was going to be a party. What was her mother going on about?

'But, Mum, Saturday's my birthday,' she protested.

'Oh, I know that, darling, of course I do,' chirruped her mother (who in truth had got confused and only remembered when she perused Holly's list in a boring bit of the committee meeting that morning). 'And of course you'll have your presents and I thought maybe a nice cake and then on Sunday you, me and Dad could go to Bella Pasta for lunch . . .'

That did it. No way, thought Holly, am I settling for a slice of chocolate sponge and a dollop of tagliatelle for my fourteenth birthday.

'Mum! I'm not a kid any more – I don't want to celebrate my birthday with my *parents*, for heaven's sake! Get real!'

Her mother raised an eyebrow, which should have been a warning to Holly. She, however, was too irate to notice.

'And anyway, you can't do this to me because Dad said I could have a party!' she shouted. 'What's more, he said I could invite loads of friends – he PROMISED!'

Her mother raised the other eyebrow.

'Oh, he did, did he?' she said.

'Yes he did,' said Holly. 'He said it was a big day and he was looking forward to it.'

Her mother sighed.

'Well, you know your father; he lives in a world of his own. I think you will find you were talking at cross-purposes. Saturday is Dunchester Battle Day. Dad seems to think you are bringing a crowd of mates along to that.'

Dunchester had been the scene of a minor skirmish during the Civil War, when a crowd of hot-headed peasants had taken a stand against a section of Cromwell's army and lost in a rather messy manner involving bodies in the blood-drenched river and limbs lying around in fields. Not content with erecting a plaque in the local church and a statue of a rather distressed-looking farmhand on the river bank, the town had in recent years turned the whole fiasco into a money-making event, with re-enactments of the battle (orchestrated, needless to say, by Holly's father), side shows and a raft race on the River Cress.

Holly's heart sank. Her father surely couldn't

have been so thick as to imagine she'd want to take her friends to that naff do.

'So what's that got to do with anything?' demanded Holly, deciding that her mother was just fishing for an excuse not to have to fork out for the food and drink. 'Just because Dad's going to spend the day playing soldiers doesn't mean I can't have a party.'

Her mother sighed.

'Holly, don't you ever take an interest in anything that goes on?' she sighed. 'I do so try to make you aware of social issues.'

And I do try to make you aware of the mess that is my life, thought Holly. Not that I get very far.

Her mother sat down on the kitchen stool.

'I told you ages ago about the protest,' she said. 'There are plans to build the new hypermarket on Swan's Meadow and if that goes ahead, they will demolish all the old warehouse buildings.'

'So?'

'So that means losing the Lowdown Centre and the crèche and everything.'

'Oh dear, oh dear, what a disaster!' said Holly sarcastically.

'Yes it would be,' said her mother fiercely. 'For scores of young mums and their children, it would be. Not everyone lives in a large house with heating and a garden, you know, and that centre is a lifeline to single mums.'

Holly looked suitably chastened.

'And so on Saturday, we're not only going to run our usual crèche, we are going to have a rally. Lots of us – mums, the committee, teachers, all sorts,' her mother finished. 'And I've thought up a slogan – "Dunchester Battle was lost in 1642 – to win the playcentre battle, we need YOU!" Good, isn't it?'

'Mind-boggling,' muttered Holly, thinking, not for the first time, that having an elderly mother carried untold risks.

'We have to fight,' said her mother. 'These youngsters must be given a future.'

What about my future? thought Holly.

'But', she said hastily, 'my party will be in the evening. After you've done all that campaigning and stuff. And I'll do all the food. And vacuum,' she added knowing how hot her mother was on blemish-free carpets. 'So you won't have to do a thing.'

Except keep well out of the way, she added silently.

Her mother shook her head.

'No, because after I've spoken at the rally –'

'You're speaking?' For a moment the shock of having a second parent threatening to do something embarrassing in public in one afternoon diverted Holly's attention from the matter in hand.

Her mother nodded eagerly.

'Yes, and we've got TV coming,' she beamed.

Heaven save us, thought Holly.

'And then, in the evening, it's the Battle Ball and guess what?'

Holly sighed. 'What?' she said. 'You are going to tap-dance on the table between courses?'

Her mother ignored her sarcasm.

'Tim Renfrew's going – you know, our MP – and I've been seated next to him.'

Holly had had enough.

'Oh great. I get it. A poxy rally, and dinner with some stuffy MP means more than your own daughter's birthday. Oh well, great.' A tear trickled down her cheek. 'I bet you never did this to the boys. I bet they had parties and things. But of course, I'm not important.'

Her mother put an arm on her shoulder.

'Oh, sweetheart, it's not that, of course you're important. But it's not like fourteen is a special birthday like going into double figures or being eighteen or anything.'

Holly grunted. 'It's special to me,' she said.

'Look, love, if we can just get the local MP on our side, we could swing this thing,' her mother continued.

'Big deal.' Holly shrugged her mother off and turned away.

'I'll tell you what,' said her mum, remembering a lecture she had heard on 'Communicating With

Your Teenager', 'why don't you have Cleo and Tansy and that nice new girl, what's her name – Jane?'

'Jade,' mumbled Holly.

'Oh yes, Jade – have them round for a video. I'll get pizzas delivered for you. That would be nice, wouldn't it?' she added in a soothing tone of voice.

Holly swung round, crying hard now.

'Oh, yes, mega nice. Mum, we had video and pizza parties when we were seven. And you can't have videos because the boys don't like the weepy ones and –'

'Boys!' Her mother's pupils dilated in a most alarming manner. 'You are not having boys round when your father and I are out.'

'Come off it, Mum! Some of my best mates are boys.'

Her mother held up a hand.

'I'm sorry, Holly, that is my final word – you are too young to be left alone with boys. Especially some of the ones you seem to find attractive.'

'Oh, that's it, slag off my friends, why don't you!' shouted Holly. 'And what do you think is going to happen? We're not stupid, you know. Just because your generation messed up.'

'It is not up for debate,' said her mother, waving her hand dismissively. 'Just you four girls or nothing.'

'I shall look like the biggest dweeb in the whole

school,' Holly wailed. 'God, Mum, you are so unbelievably selfish! Why are you being so mean? Don't you trust me?'

Her mother bit her lip. Holly saw the moment of weakness and went in for the kill.

'Or is it just that you're bored of having me around? You never really wanted me to be born, did you?'

Her mother looked pink. It was working.

'You care more about the kids at the crèche than you do about me,' she went on. 'You tell everyone that I was an afterthought – I'm just a nuisance in your life.'

Two tears rolled satisfactorily down her nose. Her mother pressed her lips together and looked distressed as Holly had hoped she would.

'Of course you're not, darling. Well, I suppose, maybe – if it was just –'

Holly held her breath. At that moment the front door bell rang. Her mother went through to the hall.

'Oh, hello, Jade, dear – come along in,' Holly heard her say, in the tone of voice mothers use when they don't want anyone to suss that ten seconds before they were screeching like a crazed parrot.

'Thanks, Mrs Vine,' said Jade, following Angela through to the kitchen. 'Hi, Holly – how was detention?'

Holly frantically signalled to her but it was too late.

'Detention?' Her mother swung round to face her. 'You told me you had netball practice. And two minutes ago you were asking me if I trusted you. That's it then – forget party. It's a video or nothing. And you're lucky to get that.'

Jade gulped and threw an apologetic glance to Holly. Holly was past caring. Her credibility was wrecked, her chances of ever getting a life as good as over.

'I just don't believe you can do this to me!' she hissed at her mother. 'I hate you – I really, really hate you!'

Angela Vine did not look particularly distressed by this outpouring of venom, but simply smiled, picked up her car keys and hurried out.

'Well, thanks a million, Jade,' snarled Holly. 'You have just ruined my birthday. I hope you're satisfied.'

WEDNESDAY

In that dark hour before the dawn. Worries . . .

Holly didn't have a very good night. When she was awake, she was worrying about what everyone would say when she told them the party was off. But when she was asleep she dreamt that Scott told her she was a total rat and went to Norwich with Ella while Trig, who refused to speak to her ever again, went off to play basketball with Cleo. She hoped that by the morning her mother would be suffering from pangs of terminal guilt and change her mind. She didn't think it was very likely.

Guilt pangs . . .
Jade's night was not exactly restful either. She felt awful for having dropped Holly in it with her mum. Not only was she worried that Holly wouldn't want her as a friend any more, but she realized with a

61

sickening thud that now there was no chance of getting Scott on his own. If only she could turn the clock back. But she couldn't. Not about anything. Holly said she was never going to speak to her mother again. But she would. Jade would never speak to hers again. She couldn't. She rolled over and buried her face in the pillow and cried.

Fantasies . . .

Tansy, meanwhile, was dreaming that she and Trig were driving along a freeway in a white Cadillac, driven by her father, who turned out to be a millionaire businessman who had always wanted a daughter. Tansy was dressed in a long scarlet evening dress with her hair, now perfectly manageable, piled on top of her head. It was just as Trig was pulling her towards him in a passionate embrace that the alarm clock woke her with a jolt. She smiled like a satisfied kitten. It didn't matter. She could find out what happened next when she got to Holly's party.

And more worries . . .

Cleo was lying on her back, staring at the ceiling and worrying. Her mum said that if they had Worrying as an event in the Olympic Games, Cleo would come away with the gold medal.

This time she was worrying about Holly's party. Well, not the party itself, actually – the sleepover bit. What if she had one of her bad dreams and shouted or screamed out? She would never live it down; just thinking about it made her shake. She was always nervous about staying over in other people's houses because she felt embarrassed if she had to go to the loo in the night and couldn't find the light switch and she sometimes slipped her thumb into her mouth when she was falling asleep and then she got teased. She would have to think of an excuse to go home after the party. Maybe she could say her dad was coming up the next morning. That would be a good one. Everyone knows that when you only get to see your dad once a month, every second counts.

Now that she had found an escape route she felt better. Of course, she didn't have anything halfway decent to wear. If only she hadn't been what her mum called pleasantly rounded, she could have borrowed some of Portia's clothes. Portia was tall, slim and very clever. She was also the sort of person who could wear a bin liner and look a million dollars.

Cleo sighed. She wondered how old you had to be to have liposuction.

9 a.m. In a foul mood

'I'm really sorry about dumping you in it last night,' said Jade to Holly as they went to Registration.

'So am I,' said Holly curtly.

'So the party really is off?' ventured Jade, hoping that something might have changed.

'Thanks to you, yes,' she snapped a trifle unfairly. 'Look, you got me into this mess so now you can just shut up, OK? Don't you dare say a single word to anyone about the party being cancelled.'

Jade's eyes widened. She had never seen Holly so angry.

'OK,' she said shortly, 'but you're going to have to tell them sometime.'

'Oh get lost!' said Holly.

And hated herself for being so horrid.

11.30 a.m. In an even more foul mood
'Hey, Holly, come shopping with me tomorrow after school? Mum's given me some cash for a new skirt!' Tansy hopped excitedly from one foot to the other.

Holly swallowed.

'Can't,' she said. 'Dentist.'

2.15 p.m. Approaching panic stations
'Great about the party, Holl!' called Ursula Newley from across the classroom. 'Me and Nick are really looking forward to it! What time?'

Holly squirmed.

'I'll let you know,' she muttered. 'Must dash.'

3.15 p.m. At the end of tether

'Er, Holly,' said Cleo nervously after Biology. 'About Saturday – I don't think I can sleep over – my dad's coming the next day and –'

'That's OK,' said Holly. 'It doesn't matter.'

Oh, thought Cleo.

And rather wished it did.

7.15 p.m. Doing the grovel – big time

'Look, Mum, I'm sorry about not telling you about detention, and I'm sorry I was horrid, and I didn't mean it. But please, please, can I have a party? Just a small one? Without food? Ending at eleven? OK, ten-thirty. Pleeeeese. No? What do you mean, no? I said I was sorry, didn't I? I hate you.'

10 p.m. In despair

I'll have to tell them. All of them. That the party's off. And they will ask why, and I will have to say that it's because my mother cares more about a handful of snotty-nosed infants and my father's dressing up in black knickerbockers and running amok with a pikestaff. I can't tell them. I have to. I will never be happy again.

THURSDAY

After lunch. Sitting by the tennis courts

'And she just wouldn't listen to reason!' Holly concluded after she had plucked up the courage to tell her mates the disastrous news.

'Look, if you want the party to happen,' said Tansy determinedly, 'you have to make it happen. You can't just sit back and say, "Oh well, that's it then."'

Not when Trig was going, you couldn't, she thought. At last she thought she was really falling in love.

'If you've got a mother like mine you can,' retaliated Holly. 'Honestly, sometimes parents are more trouble than they are worth.'

Cleo pulled a face at her, and Holly remembered Jade. Seeing her downcast expression, she felt a pang of guilt, even though she was still mad at her for wrecking everything.

Jade, in fact, was at that point not thinking about her mum but about the fact that without Holly's party as an excuse she wouldn't get to see Scott on his own. That shouldn't matter but it did. A lot. Ever since he had thrown that frisbee for his dog, Fitz, and it had landed on Jade as she sat behind a laurel bush thinking about Mum, she had thought about him all the time. He'd been so nice – he hadn't asked her what was wrong; he hadn't teased her. Just asked if she was hurt and then talked about how daft Fitz was and how he couldn't catch a frisbee to save his life. And Jade found herself telling him about the accident – and she hadn't even asked him not to tell anyone she had been crying. She just knew he wouldn't.

'Maybe your mum will change her mind,' Cleo suggested. She didn't really mind one way or the other but she hated to see people unhappy.

'Maybe pink pigs will fly past the Art block,' mumbled Holly.

'Tell me again,' said Jade slowly. 'Just why won't she let you?'

'Because', said Holly with mock patience, 'my sad father is fighting mock battles while my oh-so-noble mother waves placards and tries to save a playground. And then they are going to put on evening dress and pretend to be normal people again and go to some boring ball and suck up to politicians.'

'There has to be something we can do,' said Tansy.

'There is,' said Jade.

Everyone looked at her in surprise. Jade was usually so quiet.

'What if we all offered to help out on Saturday?' suggested Jade. 'I mean, you said she was doing a crèche and stuff – we could look after the kids, or wave a banner or something.'

'Oh, big deal,' said Holly, still miffed at Jade for messing things up in the first place. 'And that's supposed to make up for not having a party, is it? You have a weird idea of fun.'

'I get it,' said Tansy, eyes brightening. 'We trade our help for your mum's permission to have a party. Jade, that's brilliant.'

Jade looked chuffed.

'It might work,' said Holly doubtfully. 'But my mum is so hung up on boys being in the house, I can't see she'll change – and there's no point in a party without guys.'

There is when they never take any notice of you anyway, thought Cleo.

'It's worth a try,' said Tansy, clutching at straws. 'We've nothing to lose.'

6.30 p.m.

Holly did her homework in record time. She emptied the garbage, fed Naseby, and made her mother, who was trying to write her speech, a large pot of tea and a toasted teacake.

'What's all this in aid of?' asked her mother with a smile. 'Or can I guess?'

Holly took a deep breath and recited word for word what Jade had told her to say.

'I know I should have told you about the detention and I'm sorry; I was just ashamed of myself and didn't want to upset you. And I'm sorry I yelled at you. And I do understand about your evening being important. So could we compromise?'

Her mother looked impressed. Jade had said that parents warmed to the word compromise.

'What are you suggesting?'

'What if Jade and me and Cleo and Tansy all come along on Saturday to help?' Holly sat back and waited for an outpouring of maternal gratitude.

Her mother laid down her pen and eyed her quizzically.

'Well,' she said, 'that would be very nice.'

'And then, if we did, could I have a party afterwards?'

Her mother sighed.

'Oh, Holly, it's not that I want to be a killjoy,'

she said, 'but I can't let you have a party when there is no one responsible in the house to keep an eye on you. The other mothers would go spare.'

'No, no they wouldn't, honestly,' insisted Holly. 'They realize that at our age we need to extend our social horizons.' Holly remembered the phrase from a PSE worksheet and rather liked the way it rolled off the tongue.

Her mother roared with laughter which was not the idea.

'Good try, darling, but no,' she said, without a glimmer of remorse. 'Look, why not wait until half-term and have a party then? That would be nice, wouldn't it?'

Half-term is no good, thought Holly. Ella will be around at half-term. I need the party now.

'Think about it, sweetheart,' cooed her mother. 'Settle for a girlie night in. Remember, life is what you make it.'

Not when you're a teenager, it's not, thought Holly angrily. It's what your stuffy parents choose to make it.

FRIDAY

8.50 a.m. Talking boys

Dear Jade,
It was great to get your letter. This guy sounds cool – and after all, your mum and dad wouldn't want you to live like a nun for ever, would they? And remember, if other girls want this guy, that's up to them. Go for it, kiddo – and be sure to let me know how you get on.
Miss you heaps.
Oodles of love,
Tanya

'Jade?' Cleo hurled her books into her locker and turned to her friend.

'Yes?'

'Do you fancy Scott Hamill?'

'Me?' squeaked Jade. Was it that obvious? She didn't want anyone to know. 'No, why?'

'Just that you look at him a lot – and he seems quite keen on you too.'

Jade took a deep breath. Keen? Whoopee!

'Wouldn't be any point, would there?' she said, trying to sound unconcerned. 'He's going out with Ella.'

'Oh, I know he is,' agreed Cleo, 'but that's not the point. Holly used to go out with him.'

Jade didn't know that. That did it: if Scott could dump someone as stunning as Holly there was no way he'd take a second look at Jade. He was obviously just being kind to her.

'And she wants to get him back,' said Cleo. 'I mean, mega badly wants to get him back.'

'Fine,' said Jade, trying to sound disinterested. 'I'm not into boys anyway.'

'That's OK, then,' said Cleo.

No it's not, thought Jade. She could, of course, be really nice and tell Scott that Holly still fancied him. But she didn't want to. Not at all. She wanted someone in her life who was for her and her alone. She would do what Tanya said. She would go for it.

A little tingle of excitement ran down her spine. It was a new feeling.

Lunchtime. First advances

'Hi, Jade!' Scott Hamill sauntered into the library where Jade was on Returns duty.

He perched on the desk.

'How are you doing?' he asked.

'Fine,' she said, conscious that Cleo was

watching her from behind the Geography –
Europe section.

'How's Fitz?' she asked, knowing how much
Scott loved his mongrel. 'Learnt to catch frisbees
yet?'

Scott laughed.

'That dog will never learn anything – thick as
two short planks,' he said affectionately.

There was another awkward silence.

'You going to Holly's party?' he asked.

Jade nodded, trying to look casual.

'Great,' said Scott. 'I'm glad. See you around.'

And he scuttled out of the room.

He's glad, thought Jade. That must mean something. She felt a surge of happiness for the first time
in months. If Holly wanted Scott, she'd have to
fight her for him first.

2.15 p.m. More advances

'So did you get your mum to change her mind?'
Tansy asked Holly as the bell rang for afternoon
lessons.

Holly shook her head and sighed.

'So no party?' Jade asked. Typical. Just when
she had got her act together.

Holly shrugged.

'Just us four – big deal,' she sighed. 'I suppose
I'll have to tell the others.'

Cleo tried to cheer her up.

'We can still have a laugh,' she said. 'And at least the oldies won't be there to tell us to keep the noise down.'

'That's it! Cleo, you're brilliant!' Holly suddenly grinned.

'What?' chorused Tansy and Jade

'If Mum and Dad aren't there, they won't know what goes on, will they?' exclaimed Holly triumphantly. 'So we make like it's just a sleep-over and then, when they've left for the dance, we get the other guys round.'

Cleo chewed her lip.

'But what if they come back early and we get found out?' she ventured. And how do I get out of this sleepover idea?

'So – I get grounded,' admitted Holly. 'But at least we'll have had our fun and they can't take that away from us.'

Tansy nodded.

'And if we still do this oh-so-helpful bit on Saturday, and you do get found out, you just throw your mum the "after all I did for you" line that they keep hurling at us.'

Holly grinned and nodded.

'Ace!' she said. 'Spread the word with the others to come round at eight o'clock – and tell them to keep shtoom about it. That way, nothing can go wrong, can it?'

2.25 p.m. Lurking behind a locker

'Holly Vine!' Mrs Harvey, who was head of PE and whose legs would have done very well as replacements for a Chippendale chair, laid a hand on Holly's shoulder, remembered Guidelines to Teachers and took it off again. 'Why are you not getting changed for swimming?'

'I can't, please, Mrs Harvey,' lied Holly. 'Time of the month.'

'Holly, you have used that excuse for the past three Fridays. Maybe I should write to your mother suggesting a trip to the doctor.'

Holly tried again.

'Verruca,' she said, cursing the dead governor whose bounty enabled West Green Upper to be the only school in town with an indoor pool.

'Swim,' said Mrs Harvey.

Half a minute later in boys' changing rooms

'Trig Roscoe! You should be changed and in the pool by now.'

Trig smiled what he hoped was a winning smile at Mr Wynne.

'We don't swim during Fall semester in the States, sir,' he said.

Mr Wynne, a man who was absent when God handed out humour, glowered.

'It may have escaped your notice, Roscoe, that

you are not in America now, and here we do swim – all year round. Change. Now.'

Trig tried again.

'No kit, sir,' he said.

Mr Wynne was not impressed. He couldn't make the boy swim with no gear, and he did so hate to lose.

'Next week, you come fully equipped. Or take a detention.'

'Yes, sir,' replied Trig meekly, knowing full well he would opt for detention any day. Anything was better than having to endure a swimming lesson.

'Hey, Holly, what are you doing?' Holly jumped out of her skin. She was in her swimming gear, with her tracksuit top buttoned to the neck, hiding behind the benches at the end of the pool and hoping Mrs Harvey's eagle eye wouldn't spot her. The last person she expected to see was Trig.

'Ssh,' she whispered urgently. 'Don't drop me in it – I'm bunking swimming.' She looked at him. 'Why aren't you in the pool? Can't you swim?'

'Of course I can swim – pretty well, actually,' he said shortly. 'I forgot the gear. What about you? You're changed.'

Holly thought fast.

'I hate it,' she said. 'Dumb sport – and when I don't want to do something, I don't do it.'

She hoped that she sounded really chilled and in control.

'Holly Vine! Into the pool. Now. Four lengths backstroke and no arguing.'

Holly's heart stopped.

She couldn't. Bad enough at any time. But now, standing right next to Trig, who she fancied more and more each day, she couldn't.

She stared at Mrs Harvey.

'I could, of course, write to your mother!' boomed Mrs Harvey, striding towards her down the poolside, her trainers making squishing noises as she approached.

No way, thought Holly.

'Coming,' she shouted, turning her back on Trig, ripping off her tracksuit top and jumping into the water. It was so cold she caught her breath. Now all she had to do was make sure she kept well under the water and was the last out of the pool. Then maybe no one would notice how deformed she was.

3.45 p.m. Civil war
'Holly! Hang on a minute!' She turned to find Trig sprinting across the school yard towards the gate.

'Hey, Holly, can I ask you a favour?' His eyes crinkled at the edges as he gave her a lopsided grin. Holly's kneecaps began dissolving. She wished she didn't smell of chlorine.

'Of course,' she said, only it came out all squeaky and not at all deep and sophisticated as she had intended.

'Mr Eastwood has given me this history project to do – "*My favourite period in English history*".'

'Poor you,' said Holly who had had enough history rammed down her throat at home to last her a lifetime.

'I was wondering . . .' Trig paused and kicked an empty cola can with the toe of his shoe.

'Yes?' said Holly, trying to keep her heartbeat to some sort of regulation norm.

'Well, could I come round to your house and maybe ask if your dad had some info and books and stuff – I've chosen the Civil War.'

Holly gaped at him.

'You've *chosen* the Civil War?' she repeated incredulously.

Trig nodded.

'Sure have. So, will your dad mind?'

'Mind?' said Holly. 'He will probably go into paroxysms of joy. I think he feels cheated because none of his own kids actually like dead people.'

'So when can I come?' he said.

Holly was never one to waste an opportunity.

'Now?' she said.

4.05 p.m. Heading for high drama

'Neat house!' said Trig admiringly as he and Holly scrunched up the gravel drive. 'Is that the date it was built?'

He pointed to the ivy-clad wall above the bedroom windows where a diamond-shaped stone bore the figures 1884.

Holly nodded.

'I love old things,' said Trig.

'You'd better come and meet my father then!' replied Holly dryly.

When Holly pushed open the kitchen door, she stopped dead in astonishment. And horror. And then sent up a very rapid, silent prayer that the ground would open, right there, and swallow her up.

Standing in the middle of the kitchen, beaming from ear to ear, was her mother. Dressed as a white rabbit. With large floppy ears. And as if that wasn't enough, her father, wearing a tin helmet and leather jerkin, was charging the vegetable basket with a battered pikestaff.

I think, thought Holly, I am part of a very dysfunctional family.

'Darling,' said her mother, 'wonderful timing – you can tell me how I look. Oh, I'm sorry, I didn't see you had a friend. And this is . . .?'

'Trig,' said Holly, wondering if anyone else's mother was in need of certification. 'He's from

America and he wants Dad to help him with some Civil War thing he's got to write.'

Rupert Vine stopped in mid charge, adjusted his helmet and beamed with delight.

'If you don't mind, sir,' said Trig politely.

'Mind? I'd be delighted. Just let me get this manoeuvre right – one must sidestep as one thrusts, you know.'

My father should be put away somewhere very quiet, thought Holly. Her mother flicked a rabbit ear out of her face, and smiled at Trig.

'Nice to meet you, Trig,' said Angela, holding out a pink padded paw. 'Isn't this fun?' She gave a little twirl and wiggled her white cotton-wool tail. Holly decided it was time to die.

'It's for Saturday,' said her mother. 'We're dressing up,' she added for Trig's benefit.

'I get it,' said Trig. 'You're having a fancy dress do for your par –'

'Have a biscuit,' said Holly hastily, grabbing the tin off the counter top and thrusting it under Trig's nose. She knew that if Trig said the word 'party' her mother would go into overdrive.

'Your mum's a rabbit and your dad's a –'

'Roundhead, young man,' Rupert said robustly. 'It's all because of Dunchester Dozen Day. Though, of course, you don't know about that, do you? Well, you see, in sixteen forty-two at the very outset of the Civil War, twelve peasants . . .'

Holly sighed. Once her father got started, they could be here all night.

'Look, come upstairs and I'll get you some books,' said her father, leading Trig to the door.

After they had gone, Holly looked at her mother.

'I know Dad dresses up for kicks, but surely you're not going to make a speech looking like something out of *The Flopsy Bunnies*?' she asked wearily.

'Oh, darling, of course not,' said her mother. 'We doing the crèche in fancy dress and then marching to the other end of Swan's Meadow for the Rally.'

'Dressed like *that*?' gasped Holly.

'Yes, darling, we hope it will attract people's attention,' said her mother.

'You can bet on it,' observed Holly. 'I imagine the men in white coats will be hauling you away.'

Her mother pulled a face.

'Then I shall slip out of the costume and address the meeting,' said her mum. 'I am a bit nervous about it but it has to be done. These children are –'

'Our future. Yes, I know,' sighed Holly.

Holly's mother pulled off her rabbit ears and was unzipping her costume when Rupert burst into the kitchen, followed by an eager-looking Trig.

'Angela dear, where is the costume box? You know, the one with all the spare bits and pieces?'

Mrs Vine looked at him in surprise.

'In the cupboard under the stairs – why?'

'Need to kit out young Trig here,' said Rupert.

'Your dad says I can be a peasant boy,' affirmed Trig, with as much excitement as if he had just been given permission to help himself to the gold reserves at Fort Knox. 'I'm going to take part in this battle thing. On Saturday.'

'You are *what*?' Holly looked aghast.

'That young Jeffreys lad has dropped out,' said her father. 'French exchange or some such – so we are short of a bystander.'

'Dad, Trig doesn't want to get involved in –'

'Sure I do,' said Trig. 'I told you, I love this stuff.'

'Well now, I think this will do – slip your shirt off, Trig, and we'll see if it fits.' Rupert held up a peasant smock of uncertain age and somewhat strange odour.

'Er . . . no, no . . . I'll take it home and try it on there,' said Trig hastily. 'No problem.'

'As you like,' said Holly's dad, handing him some brown leggings. 'But what if it's the wrong size?'

'It will be fine,' said Trig, snatching it out of Mr Vine's hand. 'Truly.'

'So we'll see you about lunch-time,' said Mr Vine. 'Then I can show you the ropes.'

SATURDAY

Noon. On Swan's Meadow

The four girls were out of breath by the time they reached Swan's Meadow, where Dunchester Battle Day was in full swing. Holly was wearing the new red hipsters and trouser boots that her parents had given her and was smelling rather strongly of the exotic perfume that Tansy and Cleo had chosen. She hoped that the combination would have the desired effect on either Scott or Trig.

The girls pushed through the crowds and found the marquee that housed the crèche.

'Over here, dears!' Holly's mother waved frantically from inside a bright yellow playpen, her rabbit ears flopping.

The things I do to get a social life, thought Holly.

For the next two hours they made Lego houses

and pushed toddlers round on bikes and read stories and played with finger-paints. Holly was just doing battle with a three-year-old who was attempting to kill her with a plastic sword, when her mother rushed up.

'I've got to get ready for the march,' she said breathlessly. 'Can you girls take this banner over to where Dad's lot are going to do the battle scene? Tie it to a tree or something.'

Great, thought Holly. I can find Trig.

Neat, thought Tansy. I can start working on Trig.

I wonder, thought Jade, if Scott will turn up.

'Supposing we can't find a tree?' asked Cleo.

1.15 p.m.

'Isn't that your dad?' Tansy pointed to where a tall figure was instructing a group of guys on how to dismember a pretend Cavalier.

'Sadly, yes,' muttered Holly. 'And there's Trig – over there, talking to Scott.'

They knotted their banner to the fence and ran over to where the two boys were trying to persuade Scott's dog, Fitz, to give up his attempt to catch his own tail. Trig was doing his best to look like an old English peasant, although his smock looked a lot cleaner compared to when Holly last saw it.

'Happy birthday!' Scott said, grinning at Holly and yanking at Fitz's lead.

'Yeah – happy birthday,' echoed Trig.

84

Holly's neck tingled and her knees almost gave way. There was something very exciting about being keen on two guys at the same time.

'How do I look?' asked Trig. 'Historical, eh?'

'Great!' said Holly.

Dangerously kissable, thought Tansy. This is very definitely *IT*.

Holly's father strode over to them.

'Come along, Trig,' he said excitedly. 'We're about to get underway. This is no time to be chatting up the girls.'

Holly cringed. Her father was so utterly uncool and totally without shame.

'You're mad, Trig,' said Scott, as Trig followed Rupert into the arena. 'But go for it!'

They settled down on the grass to watch the proceedings. The sun was shining and it was very warm for September. Holly, who had been to loads of these things before, yawned in a bored fashion and lay back on the grass, ignoring the spectacle of her eccentric father. For some reason, her friends seemed to think the whole thing was pretty cool. The Roundheads and Cavaliers did a lot of shouting and bashing about with pikestaffs, whilst a crowd of pretend peasants with hoes and shovels marched purposefully up the hill. Then a bunch of women waved their fists and sobbed into shawls.

'Isn't that Miss Partridge?' said Tansy, pointing

to a woman dressed in a black shawl and long brown skirt who was walking unsteadily with four or five other women.

'You're right,' said Holly. 'She doesn't look as if she is totally with it. Not that there's anything unusual about that.'

Suddenly, a group of Roundheads, led by Holly's dad waving a pikestaff, charged down the slope towards the peasants. Mr Vine, getting into the mood of the occasion, yelled a few expletives in the local medieval dialect and plunged the tip of his staff towards a burly farmer. Unfortunately, the tip of the pikestaff stuck in the ground and Holly's father, still shouting, shot inelegantly into the air, over the top of his weapon and straight into Miss Partridge who collapsed to the ground in an untidy heap. Her groans were frightfully authentic – but then with all fourteen stone of Holly's father on top of her, they were unlikely to be anything else.

Cameras clicked as the photographers from the *Evening Telegraph* captured the moment.

'I don't think', said Holly, 'that was meant to happen.'

Her father rolled over and lay on the ground, motionless. A lot of Roundheads suddenly stopped being Roundheads and started having a little panic. Miss Partridge sat up and stared at Holly's dad.

'Oh dear,' she said. And fainted.

The photographers were having a field day.

It was when Mr Vine tried to stand up, blood pouring from his nose, and fell instantly back to the ground that Holly realized this was serious.

'Dad's hurt!' cried Holly. 'Scott, go and get Mum! She's waiting for the march to start. Down by the river.'

'OK,' said Scott, jumping up, snatching Fitz's lead and heading off down the hill. Jade hesitated for one moment and then sped after him, much to Cleo's annoyance.

'We need to stop the bleeding,' shouted someone. 'And his ankle looks as if it might be broken. Get the St John's Ambulance up here now!'

A young reporter, notebook in hand, sped over to the scene, scribbling as he ran. Holly's heart raced. She ran over to her father, her two friends close on her heels. Trig was hovering some distance away, chewing his lip.

'You, lad!' shouted someone. 'Give us your shirt.'

Trig froze.

'Come on, boy, for heaven's sake – quickly.'

Trig stood motionless, his gaze averted from where Holly's dad lay on the ground.

'Trig!' Cleo snapped. 'Get on with it!'

Trig glanced at her, pulled off his shirt, threw it at the man and ran off.

Holly and Tansy looked at him in amazement.

'What's up with Trig?' asked Tansy.

Before Holly could reply, two bustling St John's

Ambulance men arrived and set about examining Rupert's still bleeding nose. Then they strapped up his foot and lifted him into the vehicle, followed by a slowly reviving Miss Partridge, who kept saying 'Oh dear' somewhat ineffectually.

'Dad – Scott's gone to get Mum!' said Holly, leaning over her father.

'No need, no need,' he said bravely. 'She's got her march – I'm fine. Just a bit of a knock. Tell her I'll see her in Casualty when she's done her speech. And wish her luck.'

'I'll come with you,' said Holly.

Her father shook his head.

'Enjoy the day,' he said. 'It is your birthday after all. And say sorry to Trig for spoiling his fun, won't you?'

Holly nodded and turned to find him.

But Trig had gone.

2.55 p.m. Trying to be cool

'Excuse me, but did I hear you say that guy was your father?' The young reporter, pen poised, grinned at Holly. 'Don't look so worried, he'll be fine.'

'He wasn't rambling or incoherent or anything,' said Tansy comfortingly. 'Which means his mind is OK.'

'Makes a change,' said Holly with a watery smile.

'I'm Leo Bellinger, from the *Evening Telegraph*,' said the reporter. 'Now, could you give me a few details . . .'

'Sorry,' said Holly, 'can't stop. I have to find my mother – she's speaking at the rally in a minute.'

'Really?' The reporter pocketed his notebook. 'I'll try and catch that – two people in the same family making the headlines – great!' He beckoned to the photographer and the two of them dashed off.

Holly scanned the crowds.

'Where is Scott? He should have found Mum by now.'

'And where's Trig?' questioned Tansy.

'I think he was embarrassed,' said Cleo. 'I saw he had this huge birthmark all over his chest.'

'Oh . . . how unsexy,' commented Holly. Maybe I'll go for Scott instead, she thought.

Cleo stared at her.

'Looks aren't everything,' she said, surprising herself. Not that she liked Trig that much or anything, but she couldn't help thinking about how miserable he looked. And she hated to see anyone unhappy. And when he wasn't posing he looked – well, more lovable.

'Look,' said Tansy, pointing across the field. 'There's your mum.'

Holly stopped dead in her tracks.

'Oh no, please, please no,' she breathed.

Standing behind a table on a wooden platform with a microphone in one paw was a large white rabbit. And everyone in the crowd was laughing. A cameraman from TV East was focusing his lens on her white bobtail.

'She's supposed to have changed into a dress or something,' wailed Holly. 'I can't bear it!'

They stood on a bench to get a better view. Everyone was still laughing and Holly spotted Leo the reporter, leaning against a nearby tree and scribbling frantically.

Holly's mum held up a paw.

'Go on, please, do laugh,' she said fiercely to the crowd. 'It is, I agree, amusing that the zip has broken and I am stuck in this costume for the foreseeable future.'

The crowd chuckled, but it was a kinder chuckle this time.

'Your laughter can't hurt me,' declared Mrs Vine. 'But let the developers knock down the day centre and you can hurt a lot of young people who need our support – young people who have very little to laugh about.'

'She's good,' whispered Tansy.

'She's amazing,' agreed Cleo.

'This is one heck of a story,' said the reporter, flipping over a page.

Holly opened one eye. She had to admit that her mum sounded pretty in command.

'Would you sleep easy in your bed at night knowing that you had done nothing to save a day centre that gives support to the disadvantaged, just so that you could have yet another hypermarket?'

A murmur went through the crowd. The cameraman moved closer and beckoned to a girl in a green jacket carrying a furry mike. Holly opened the other eye.

'Fight the closure,' stormed Mrs Vine, waving a white furry arm in the air. 'Because if you don't you are condemning a lot of young people to a life on the streets.' Applause echoed round the crowd.

'Get a picture of that woman, Jack.' Leo obviously couldn't believe his luck. Holly felt quite proud, and began to edge forward so that she could let her mum know about the accident.

Mrs Vine turned to the table, and took a sip from a glass of water, which was difficult through several centimetres of fur and wire whiskers.

Just then, a tall man with a big moustache, wearing a waxed jacket and green moleskin trousers, pushed to the front of the crowd and jumped on to the platform.

'Good riddance to the layabouts, that's what I say! Glue-sniffing, no-good wasters, that's all they are!'

Mrs Vine wheeled round to face the heckler, her rabbit ears bouncing up and down.

'What did you say?'

Saturday

The man repeated it louder and more aggressively.

Mrs Vine drew herself to her full height, took three steps forward and threw the glass of water in his face. And then the entire contents of the jug. The man gasped, staggered around the platform and almost caught hold of Mrs Vine's flapping rabbit ears.

'No!' cried Holly involuntarily. Stop it, Mum. Please.

It would have been all right if her mum had been wearing shoes. But little pink padded paws are very slippery and as she stepped backwards to avoid the angry heckler, she slid on the spilt water and shot over the edge of the platform, landing on top of the young policeman who had spent all morning feeling bored.

The audience gasped. The photographer, unable to believe his luck, took picture after picture. Holly considered putting herself up for adoption.

The constable, who was supposed to be on crowd control but was hoping for a real crime, decided that, in the absence of bank robbers on the run or a defecting spy, he supposed a deranged woman would have to suffice.

'Come along now, madam, I think it's time we finished up, don't you?' he said, picking himself up and trying to look dignified, despite being covered in bits of grass and the odd lump of nylon rabbit fur.

'Don't you patronize me!' shouted Holly's mum.

The TV crew moved in closer.

Holly shut both eyes again. The shame of it all. She heard her friends gasp.

She opened them. The policeman's helmet was on the grass and Mrs Vine was being marched ceremoniously towards a white van with POLICE in large letters on the side, followed by the camera crew and the reporter.

It's OK, thought Holly. In a moment I'll wake up. It's all a nightmare.

She ran up to the van, closely followed by Cleo and Tansy.

'Mum!' she cried.

Mrs Vine turned round and waved.

'Not to worry, sausage!' she called. 'No problem.'

Oh great, thought Holly. You call me sausage in public, get arrested and then say there's no problem.

'Just tell your father what's happened, there's a love.'

'But, Mum –'

The van door shut.

Holly suddenly felt very small and burst into tears. She hadn't managed to tell her mum about her dad and her dad wouldn't know her mum was in custody and she didn't know what to do.

'Don't cry, love,' said the reporter. 'They'll let her out after they've given her a caution. It's only a formality.'

Formality or not, Holly felt miserable. Trig was nowhere to be seen and Scott had disappeared too. Her birthday wasn't turning out at all the way she imagined.

3.20 p.m. What next?

Holly, Cleo and Tansy were just wondering what to do next when Jade came rushing up to them, out of breath and flushed in the face.

'Have you seen Fitz?' she gasped, brushing a strand of honey-coloured hair out of her eyes.

'Who's Fitz?' asked Tansy, wondering if this was yet another dishy guy she had hitherto overlooked.

'Scott's dog,' explained Jade. 'He broke loose from his lead when Scott was looking for Holly's mum – did you find her, by the way?'

'Not exactly,' said Holly and told Jade the whole story.

'That's awful,' said Jade. 'Are you going to the police station to find your mum? Because if you are, I'll come too and report Fitz lost.'

'That's a great idea,' agreed Holly. 'Where is Scott? He ought to come too.'

'He's down by the river asking people if they've seen anything,' said Jade.

She paused.

'Poor thing, he's in pieces about it. I'd love to be able to find Fitz for him.'

Holly stared at her. And it hit her like a stone. Jade fancied Scott too. Well, tough. Jade had already blown the chance of a proper party, so she certainly wasn't going to get Scott. Holly was going to make quite sure of that.

'What's your relationship to the dog's owner, dear?' The policewoman looked up from filling in the lost-property form. 'Girlfriend, are you?'

'No she's not, she's just his friend,' interrupted Holly instantly. 'We are all friends of his.'

DUNCHESTER POLICE
LOST-PROPERTY REPORT

Item lost . . . . *one mongrel – male, brown and white, short-haired, scruffy. Answers to the name of Fitz. Last seen Swan's Meadow 20 September*

Owner . . . . *Scott Hamill, 2 Dulverton Road, Oak Hill, Dunchester*

Person reporting loss . . *Miss Jade Williams, 53 Lime Avenue, Oak Hill, Dunchester*

Relationship . . . .

At that moment a side door opened and Holly's mother emerged, looking extremely cheerful for someone who had been on the wrong side of the law. Holly rushed up to her and gave her a big hug, for once not minding what her friends thought.

'Holly darling! What are you doing here? And all your friends! What a day – people did notice me, didn't they?'

'Notice you? Mum, the whole thing was filmed by TV East.'

Her mother clapped her hands in delight.

'Brilliant!' she cried. 'Couldn't be better!'

She caught the eye of the police officer on the desk.

'Only of course I didn't mean it to end like that – very silly of me,' she said, sounding as if she didn't mean a word of it. 'Dad outside with the car, is he?'

'No, he's in hospital because . . .'

'Hospital!' Her mother grabbed the edge of the desk and turned pale. 'What –?'

'Don't worry, Mrs Vine, it's not serious,' said Cleo at once.

'He pole-vaulted over his pikestaff and hurt his ankle,' said Tansy.

'And his nose bled like anything – Miss Partridge fainted and Trig . . .' Holly gabbled.

'I must get to the hospital at once,' said Mrs Vine.

'I'll come with you,' offered Holly.

'No, dear, you go home,' said her mother. 'And can you phone Mrs Heatherington-Smythe?'

'Why?'

'Well, if your father is hurt, we won't be going to the ball tonight, will we? And she'll need to make a few changes of plan on the top table.'

The girls looked at one another, all thinking the same thing.

If Holly's parents didn't go to the ball, it wasn't just Mrs Heatherington-Smythe who would be changing her plans.

4.15 p.m. *The seed of an idea*

'What are we going to do?' asked Holly as they walked home along Riverbank Road. 'Scott and Trig and the others will be turning up at eight o'clock and if my parents haven't gone out, all hell will break loose.'

Tansy frowned.

'But if they are at home, they won't mind you having boys round,' she reasoned.

'The fact that I had arranged it all without telling them will cause my mother to do a major flip,' said Holly. 'And believe me, that is not a pretty sight.'

Jade paused before crossing the road.

'If Scott hasn't found Fitz, there is no way he will come to the party anyway,' she said. 'He'll just spend all evening hunting for him. And if he does that Trig is bound to stay and help him.' And so will I, she added silently.

'But it's my birthday!' Holly stressed, her heart sinking. Scott had to come. And Trig. She was pretty sure it was Scott she wanted, especially now she knew Jade was after him – but then again, if that didn't work out, there was always Trig to fall back on.

'And Fitz is Scott's dog!' retorted Jade. 'He could be hurt or locked in somewhere or anything. An animal's life matters more than your stupid party.'

Holly glared at her. She didn't want anything diverting Scott's mind from falling in love with her.

An idea slowly formed in her mind. An idea that would make it certain that Scott came along. It might just work. Of course, it wasn't exactly honest – but then again, all was fair in the cause of love. Wasn't it?

'I wonder what happened to Trig,' Tansy said casually after she and Holly had waved goodbye to Cleo and Jade.

She hadn't been able to get him out of her mind all afternoon. When he had pulled off his shirt and run away, she had realized just what it was that made him so attractive. It wasn't just the blond wavy hair and those incredible liquid eyes. It wasn't even his bouncy confidence. It was the fact that she was quite certain that Trig had something secret in his life, something that all his bravado and teasing was a cover-up for. He was actually quite vulnerable and sensitive.

'He probably joined up with Scott after the accident,' said Holly. 'Guys always stick together. He'll turn up.'

6.00 p.m. Drastic events call for drastic actions

'Is that the *Evening Telegraph*? Oh good. This is Holly Vine speaking. Can I speak to Leo Bellinger, please? Yes, yes, I'll hold.'

Holly closed her eyes and sent a prayer speeding heavenwards.

'Oh, hi, it's Holly Vine – you took pictures of my mum and dad . . . yes, that's right, the Roundhead and the Rabbit. That's going to be the headline? On the front page?'

The shame of it all.

'Well, anyway, I thought you'd like to know that my mum is going to be at the Battle Ball tonight trying to persuade our MP to join her campaign. Well, no, she doesn't always throw jugs of water around, but she is quite . . . volatile.'

Holly's love of English meant that when pressed she could always find the right word for the moment.

'Oh yes, I think there might be a great story there . . . You were thinking of going? Oh do . . . Yes, she has a few tricks up her sleeve . . . All right then . . . Oh, you're welcome.'

She hung up. Stage one completed with success.

6.27 p.m. *The scheming continues*

She had just changed into her navy suede miniskirt and was trying without great success to put her hair up, when she heard a car scrunching to a halt on the gravel drive.

She ran downstairs to see her mother climbing out of a taxi.

'Hi, Mum! How's Dad?' she called.

'Not so bad, not so bad,' said her mother, handing a five-pound note to the driver and picking up her bag. 'But they are keeping him in overnight, just to be on the safe side.'

Yes! said Holly to herself. One parent dealt with, one to go.

'Come on in, Mum, and I'll make you a cup of tea,' offered Holly in her most soothing tone.

She eyed the kitchen clock. 6.30. Cleo, Tansy and Jade would be arriving at seven, and she had a lot to get sorted before then. She had to word this next bit very carefully.

'And when you've had your tea, I'll run you a bath,' she said.

Her mother shook her head.

'No, darling, I'm just going to sink into a chair and do nothing for a couple of hours.' She yawned expansively.

Oh no you are not, Mother dear, thought Holly.

'Why don't we cut your birthday cake?' her mum suggested. 'It's in the larder – I did the chocolate layer one you like so much.'

'You did? That's so nice of you!' exclaimed Holly, genuinely chuffed that her mum had remembered.

'But, Mum,' she added hastily, in wide-eyed innocence, 'what about the ball? And Tim Whatever – you know, the MP? I mean, after your triumph today you can't pass up the opportunity of meeting him.'

Her mother shrugged.

'It's a shame, I'll admit it,' she agreed, 'but Mrs Heatherington-Smythe will have found someone to take my . . . you *did* remember to phone her, didn't you?'

Holly clamped her hand to her mouth in mock horror.

'Oh, Mum, I forgot – I'm so sorry. You see, what with worrying about Dad, and talking to the reporter . . .'

'Reporter? What reporter?'

Holly regaled her mother with the story of meeting Leo at the showground and how he thought that Dad's chivalry and Mrs Vine's social

101

awareness would make a wonderful story.

'And he phoned to say he's going to be at the Ball tonight to hear that MP man speak,' said Holly. 'And he wants to do a big piece on your campaign.'

Well, twisting the truth just a little didn't matter when it was in a good cause. And there was no better cause than her party.

'Well, I don't know,' began her mother, but Holly noticed that she was drinking her tea rather rapidly and eyeing the clock. 'I suppose I could go – but without Dad . . .'

'He would hate to think you had passed up an opportunity like this, just because he was in hospital,' said Holly emphatically. 'And you did say that saving the centre was very important. But it's up to you.'

It was with great satisfaction that Holly watched her mother scoot upstairs to the bathroom.

7.25 p.m. We can't - can we?
'And she's really gone?' Tansy's eyes lit up as she flung her sleeping bag on to the floor of Holly's bedroom.

Holly nodded.

'Brilliant!' said Tansy. 'What's happened to Jade and Cleo?'

'They should be here soon,' said Holly. 'Which is why we need to get a move on. I need your help.'

'Do you want me to put out crisps and stuff?' offered Tansy.

Holly shook her head.

'No, it's much more important than that. Jade says that if Scott doesn't find Fitz, he won't come to the party. So this is what I thought . . .' And she told Tansy her plan.

Tansy's eyes widened.

'But that would be a total lie!' she gasped.

Holly stared at her.

'You were the one who said that if you wanted something enough you had to make it happen,' she insisted.

Tansy nodded slowly.

'And I suppose it wouldn't really do any harm, would it?' she said.

'So?'

Tansy thought. Where Scott went, Trig was bound to follow. And no one was interested in Trig except Tansy.

'Yes – let's go for it!' she said.

7.40 p.m. Lying through her teeth

'Hi, may I speak to Scott, please? Holly. Holly Vine.'

She covered the mouthpiece and gave the thumbs-up sign to Tansy.

'Scott, it's me – Holly. Have you found Fitz? No? Well, listen, I don't know whether this is any help but Tansy and me both think we've seen him. Running through my back garden.'

She held her breath.

'Pardon . . .? Well, sort of white with browny-black bits . . . It is? Yes, come straight away. Must go, some of the others are arriving.'

She replaced the receiver and grinned at Tansy.

'Is Trig coming with him?' asked Tansy anxiously.

'Don't know,' shrugged Holly. 'But Scott is and that will do for starters.'

8.10 p.m. Hanging in there

Within half an hour, the sitting room was full of people. Nick and Ursula were entwined round one another in one corner, apparently competing for the longest kiss in the universe competition, and Alex Gregson was rifling through Holly's collection of CDs and tapes. Cleo was sitting on the arm of a chair watching him and wishing she could think of something mind-blowingly witty to say. Jade kept going to the back door and peering into the garden, because Holly had told her that Scott's dog had been spotted in the shrubbery and she rather thought she wanted to be the one to find him.

The doorbell rang.

'Hi Holly, have you found him?' Scott, breath-less and red in the face, scanned the front garden hopefully. Trig hovered behind him, staring at the gravel with deep concentration.

'Well, no – but I'm sure he's around here some-where,' she said. 'Why don't we go into the garden and have a good look?' Amongst other things, she added silently in her head.

'I'll help,' said Trig, still not looking anyone in the eye.

'Oh, no,' interrupted Tansy. 'I don't think too many people should go searching. It might frighten him off,' she improvised quickly.

She grinned at Trig.

'Come through and I'll get you a drink,' she said, praying that the fifty minutes she had spent getting the Smouldering Chestnut eyeshadow and Purple Passion lip-liner just right would pay off.

Trig followed Tansy, rather more reluctantly than she would have liked, and Holly took Scott into the back garden. She was just about to start the first chat-up line from *Sugar*'s 'Get Your Guy' supplement, when Jade appeared at her elbow.

'Any luck?' she said brightly.

If you'd disappear, I might have, thought Holly. She sighed as Jade and Scott began peering behind bushes and prodding undergrowth.

'He might be on the building site,' suggested Jade. 'He could be stuck somewhere.'

And with that she headed through the gap in the fence, closely followed by Scott. Holly had an over-whelming desire to throttle her. If she went too, she would ruin her new shoes. If she didn't, Jade might get her mitts on Scott. On balance, the shoes would have to suffer.

8.20 p.m. Love hurts

Tansy had never seen Trig so subdued before. She had tried all the best flirting techniques she knew, but all he did was sip his cola and answer her in monosyllables. There was nothing for it: she would have to come straight to the point.

'What's wrong?' she asked, looking him straight in the eye. 'Is it something to do with this afternoon?'

Trig coloured and turned to look out of the window.

'I'd better get out there and help Scott,' he muttered, heading for the door. 'I wasn't going to bother coming to a dumb party anyway.'

'Wait!' said Tansy, grabbing his arm. She was desperate to make the most of this moment alone.

Trig shrugged her off.

'I guess I'll go home soon,' he said. 'There's baseball on Sky Sports.'

'You can't do that,' gasped Tansy. 'We've only just started.' Or in our case, not started, she thought. 'Anyway, you want to get to know everyone, don't you?'

Trig shrugged.

'I guess they won't want to get to know me – not

after, well, you know, running off like that. And anyway,' he added, looking straight at her, 'what's the point of a party when there's no chance with the girl you really like?'

Tansy's heart did a double flip with pike.

'But there is a chance, you know,' she said softly. 'A very good chance indeed.'

Trig stared at her.

'There is? Do you really mean that? Even though . . . well, despite everything?'

Tansy nodded, imagining the long, slow, lingering kiss that, if she played it right, would follow in about twenty seconds.

'Oh yes,' she breathed, hoping she sounded huskily sexy. 'Very definitely.'

This was it. She was falling in love. It was happening.

'So should I tell her how much I fancy her? Right now?'

Tansy's eyes widened.

'Tell – who?' she quavered.

'Cleo – should I tell her I think she's incredible?'

'Tell her what you like,' snapped Tansy, and went to the loo. Loos are pretty good places for people whose hearts are breaking.

8.40 p.m. Secrets on the stairs
'Hi,' said Trig, sidling up to Cleo who was sitting on the bottom of the stairs feeling fat and wishing it

was time to go home. 'I brought you some crisps.'

Cleo looked up in surprise.

'Thanks,' she said. There was no doubt about it – Trig might be a world-class bragger but he did have the most beautiful eyes.

'Has Scott found the dog?' asked Cleo, shouting over the persistent beat of jungle music.

'They're still out in the garden looking,' replied Trig. 'I want to ask you something,' he added in a rush.

Cleo looked at him questioningly.

'Will you go out with me?'

Cleo gasped.

'Pardon?' she said.

'OK, OK, I get it! It was dumb of me to ask anyway!' Trig stood up and headed down the hall.

'Hang on,' Cleo called after him. 'Give me a chance.'

Trig paused.

'I thought . . . I mean, what about these girls in the States? You said . . .'

'OK, so I lied,' he said. 'There are no girls. There never were any girls. I guess there never will be.'

Cleo stared at him. And realized that Trig was really upset.

'Tell me,' she said gently.

'Where do I begin?' asked Trig.

'Try the beginning,' said Cleo.

8.50 p.m. Last-ditch attempt

'It's getting dark,' said Holly. 'Let's go in.'

And then I get you to myself, she thought, eyeing Scott with longing.

'You go,' muttered Scott. 'I'll just go and check round once more.'

'Oh, come on,' said Holly, who was feeling desperate. 'Don't be such a party-pooper!'

Scott turned on her.

'My dog matters far more than your stupid party,' he said, his voice wobbling. 'Just go, why don't you? You'll stay, won't you, Jade?'

'Course I will,' agreed Jade.

Holly got the distinct feeling that she had made a bad move.

8.55 p.m. So this is love . . .

'I'm sorry, really I am.' Scott was sitting on an upturned wheelbarrow close to tears. 'I suppose you think I'm pretty wet, getting upset over a missing dog, especially when . . . well, compared with what you lost and all that,' he added, not certain quite how to put it.

Jade shook her head and smiled.

'Of course I don't,' she declared. 'Love is love – what or who you love doesn't come into it. You're worried sick about Fitz and I'm missing Mum and Dad – it's still pain.'

109

'Do you know something?' said Scott softly, leaning towards her.

'What?' asked Jade.

'You are lovely,' said Scott. And gently kissed her forehead.

It was very nice.

'Would you . . . I mean, suppose we went out together sometime? If you don't mind, that is.'

'I don't mind,' said Jade. 'I don't mind one little bit.'

At which point Scott kissed her again. This time on the lips. For quite a long time. So this, thought Jade, as little electric shocks galloped up and down her spine, was what falling in love was all about.

9.00 p.m. Gee!

'I've never talked to a girl like this before,' said Trig, looking embarrassed. 'In fact, I've never talked to anyone like this before.'

He had told Cleo how he had been born with a huge strawberry-coloured birthmark which spread all over his chest and back, across his shoulders and down the tops of his arms. Even though he was having treatment, it would never disappear completely, which was why he wore polo-neck sweaters and long sleeves all the time.

She discovered that he had an elder brother who had won a sports scholarship to an American university and a sister who was brilliant at athletics.

'My dad thinks they are the greatest,' he had said ruefully. 'He keeps on at me to get involved in sport and says I'm a weed and a wimp. He says he doesn't know how an ex-Marine like him could produce a runt like me. But because I hate the idea of people staring at me, I've never got involved in sports.'

'I understand,' said Cleo. 'Surely your dad does too?'

'He says I have to learn to be a real man. He skis, and shoots, and does white-water rafting – the whole bit.'

'So?' said Cleo. 'That doesn't mean you have to like that stuff.'

'But real cool guys are into that kinda thing,' said Trig. 'And what with having a hideous body –'

Cleo had had enough.

'Your body is not hideous!' she exclaimed. 'Trig, you've got a birthmark. A mark, that's all it is. I'm really sorry but it's no big deal. It's just skin, not the real you. You're a nice guy – a really nice guy,' she added, suddenly realizing that she meant every word of it. 'Especially when you stop pretending,' she added.

Trig gave a half smile.

'Oh yeah,' he drawled. 'But no girls ever fancy me when they see . . . well, you know . . .'

'What you mean', said Cleo 'is that you imagine that just because you've got a birthmark, no one

111

will fancy you. That's crazy. Holly fancies you,' she added hastily, worrying that she was coming on too strong.

'It's not Holly I'm interested in,' he said. 'It's you I asked to go out with me. But you don't want to.'

'Who says I don't?' demanded Cleo, her conscience clear now she had got the Holly thing out of the way. 'In fact, I can't think of anything nicer.'

Trig grinned. And this time it was a real grin.

'Gee,' he said.

Gee indeed, thought Cleo.

9.10 p.m. Found out

'Did you find him, Scott?' Ursula unwrapped herself from round Nick long enough to shout the question above the music as Scott and Jade came into the room, adding to the lumps of mud which Holly had trodden all over the carpet.

Scott shook his head and looked miserable. Tansy, who had got bored with sitting in the loo, turned to Alex Gregson, who was demolishing a dish of peanuts at record speed.

'Hardly surprising,' she muttered. 'Holly made the whole thing up just to get Scott over here.'

It was unfortunate that this remark was made at precisely the moment when the music stopped.

'You did *what*?' Scott wheeled round to face Holly.

'So you never really saw Fitz at all?' Jade looked incredulous.

'And I've been wasting all this time here when I could have been looking all over for him,' shouted Scott. 'Well, thanks a bunch, Holly! I'm leaving.'

Holly felt sick. She knew she'd been a total idiot, and mean, and selfish – but she couldn't bear being made to look a dweeb in front of all her friends.

'Hey, don't go!' she said. 'The party's about to hot up.'

'You are unbelievable!' shouted Scott, wrenching open the door into the hall.

Holly followed him out of the room.

'Scott, don't! I didn't . . .'

She paused as she heard a car pull up outside. Mum! She was back. She couldn't be.

Scott grabbed his denim jacket off the coat hook and pulled open the front door.

'Get lost!' he yelled at Holly, and careered out of the door, straight into Mrs Vine who was standing on the step in her peacock-blue cocktail dress, grappling with her door key.

She did not look happy. As Scott mumbled an apology and ran down the drive, she stepped into the hall, her eyes widening at the persistent beat of music echoing around the house.

'Holly,' she said, in those ominous measured tones that mothers use just before they explode in fury, 'what is going on?'

Holly's heart sank to below floorboard level. What possessed her mum to come home so early?

'I, er . . . we . . . well, you see . . .' began Holly, praying that her mother would hold back on the exploding front until they were on their own.

She didn't.

'You were told specifically that you could have the girls over for the evening,' she said, marching over to the stereo and switching it off. A deathly hush fell over the room and people stopped dancing in mid-jig. 'You were also told that boys were not allowed.'

Ursula tittered. Alex spluttered into his hand. Holly hoped that death would be rapid.

'Mrs Vine?' Cleo stood up. 'Actually, it wasn't really Holly's fault.'

Mrs Vine's eyebrows elevated.

'You see, Scott has lost his dog and Holly thought she had seen it in your garden so he came over with Trig and the others –' At this point she gave them all a 'stick to this story or else' stare – 'to help hunt for him. Only we didn't find him, and most of us have to phone for lifts from our parents to get home so we decided to play music till they came.'

Holly, Tansy and Jade stared at her. Cleo, quiet, anxious, correct Cleo, had told a lie to save her friend. Cleo was equally stunned at her actions.

She would never have believed she could speak out like that.

Trig looked at her in admiration. He took a deep breath.

'No, ma'am, it's my fault really. When Scott said Holly had seen Fitz, I rounded up the guys to help us search – I guess we never thought about asking if it was OK.'

Cleo squeezed his hand.

Mrs Vine eyed them all intently.

'I see,' she said, mellowing slightly. 'Well, I suggest you all have a slice of Holly's birthday cake and then I will drive you all home.'

'Mum!' cried Holly. 'We told their parents to come at 10.30 and . . .'

She stopped. She knew she'd blown it.

'You did? So you knew in advance about this search party for this missing dog, did you?' her mother said through gritted teeth.

She turned to the gang.

'Coats. On. Now.'

No one argued.

10.00 p.m. A life in ruins
Holly stood in the kitchen in floods of tears. Tansy put an arm round her shoulder.

'I'm really sorry,' she said. 'I didn't mean any-one to hear what I was saying. I was just in a bad mood.'

Holly sniffed.

'It's not that,' she said. 'It's just that I wanted this to be the best party ever. I wanted Scott and Trig and everyone to think I was really cool and it's all gone wrong. Scott hates me, Jade's gone home in a huff and Trig completely ignored me.'

'And me,' sighed Tansy.

Holly stared at her.

'Do you fancy Trig?'

Tansy nodded.

'Much good it did me,' she said. 'He's besotted with Cleo. And now Scott's gone off with Jade – you wanted him back, didn't you?'

Holly nodded.

'Or Trig . . . or, I suppose, anyone,' she said, suddenly realizing that it was not the guys she wanted for their own sake, but just so that she could say she had a boyfriend. And Trig and Cleo had stood up for her, even though she'd been pathetic. They were real friends, regardless of who they fancied. She saw that now.

'I just don't know how my mum could be so embarrassing, treating me like that in front of everyone,' sighed Holly. 'If only she hadn't decided to come home early. I just don't know what I'm going to do.'

'You can start, my girl, by washing the mud off the sitting-room carpet.' Her mother appeared at the kitchen door. 'Tansy dear, how nice that

116

you're staying. You could have asked Cleo,' she added, turning to Holly.

'Her dad's coming up early tomorrow so she had to go home,' said Holly.

Her mother nodded.

'Well,' she said, 'I shan't say any more about this incident, Holly, except to remind you that there are rules in life which have to be followed. And if you don't learn them at home, how are you ever going to be a reliable member of the community?'

'That's rich', said Holly, 'coming from a woman who got arrested while dressed as an overgrown rabbit.'

Her mother tried not to laugh.

She opened her arms.

'I'm sorry, Mum,' said Holly, giving her a hug. 'Really.'

'Me too,' said Tansy. 'Sorry, Mrs Vine.'

'Let's have some birthday cake,' said Holly's mum. 'And tomorrow we can celebrate with a slap-up meal and have a really relaxing day. Now, isn't that a nice idea?'

SUNDAY

9 a.m. More shared secrets

Holly and Tansy didn't wake up till nine o'clock because they had talked for hours before going to sleep. Tansy had told Holly how she wanted to be rich and famous and find her father, and Holly had told Tansy how she wanted to be shorter.

'On balance,' Tansy had said, 'I think I stand a better chance of getting my wish. You try being tiny like me – it's a total pain. I had to get my skirt in the kids' department of a clothes shop – but don't you dare tell anyone!'

'My boobs aren't doing what they should,' Holly had confessed. 'One's bigger than the other.'

'Really? No one would ever notice. Anyway, I saw this programme in Biology and it said that lots of girls have lopsided boobs in their teens. At least you've got a chest, which is more than I have.'

Holly felt better.

'But it would be nice to be utterly gorgeous – like Ella – wouldn't it?' she said.

'Well,' Tansy had murmured, just before falling asleep, 'she may have legs up to her armpits but she hasn't got a guy any more, has she? Which just goes to show that there's hope for you and me yet.'

9.45 a.m.
On Sunday morning Mrs Vine left Holly and Tansy eating their breakfast and went to the hospital to fetch her husband.

'Just don't do anything catastrophic while I'm gone,' she admonished them.

'As if,' said Holly. Her mother had only been gone about five minutes when the doorbell rang.

Standing on the front step, with William on one hip and a towelling holdall in his hand, was her brother Richard.

'Mum in?' he asked, pushing past Holly into the hall.

'*Hi, Holly. Did you have a good birthday, Holly? So sorry I forgot to send you a present, Holly. Here's a tenner to make up for it, Holly,*' chanted his sister.

'Birthday? Oh cripes, yes. Sorry, Holly – sort it with you later. Look, where's Mum?'

'Gone to the hospital to fetch Dad,' she said. 'She won't be long.'

Richard tutted.

119

'That's too bad. Nothing serious, I hope,' he said. 'Look, you'll have to take William – I've got to go to Leicester.'

'What on earth for?' asked Holly, as Richard thrust William into her arms.

'Serena's there – at her mum's – and she wants to come home,' he said triumphantly. 'Look, I've put toys and biscuits and stuff in the bag. I'll . . . we'll get back as quickly as we can. Must dash.'

'You'll have to pay me!' said Holly. 'And I don't come cheap!'

'Fine,' said her brother. And with that he hurtled through the front door and into his dilapidated Renault 5.

'Bye bye,' said William, waving his chubby hand at the closed door. 'Bikky?' he added hopefully.

'He's so cute,' said Tansy. 'Can I stay for a bit and play with him?'

'Whatever turns you on,' said Holly.

10.15 a.m. Child-minding crisis
Half an hour later, the bell rang. Holly went to the door with William padding after her.

'Remember me?' Leo, the reporter from the *Evening Telegraph*, stood grinning on the doorstep. 'Wondered if I could come in and have a word with your parents? Get a bit of background colour for this piece I'm doing.'

'Doddy,' said William, leaning out of the doorway excitedly.

'Be quiet, William,' hissed Holly. 'They're not here,' she said to Leo. 'Mum's fetching Dad from the hospital. But you can come in if you like – they'll be back soon.'

She was about to shut the front door when a sleek racing-green Jaguar pulled up the drive. An overweight man in a pinstriped suit stepped out.

'Good morning, good morning,' he boomed, holding out a hand. 'Tim Renfrew, MP for Dunchester West. Is Angela Vine about?'

'Doddy, doddy,' said William, jumping up and down and banging Holly on the knee.

Holly ignored him and repeated the story.

'But do please come through,' she said politely. 'This is Leo Bellinger from the *Evening Telegraph*. He's a reporter.'

Tim Renfrew looked as though he had just been introduced to a small and rather muddy earthworm.

'Oh, I know Mr Bellinger,' he growled, his already red face diffusing with even more colour. 'Our paths have regrettably crossed before. This whippersnapper besmirched my good name.'

Leo tried a friendly smile.

'Oh, come, Mr Renfrew,' he said, 'I was only doing my job. I only gave the people the facts.'

The MP snorted and sank into an armchair. Leo

placed himself as far away as he could. Tansy, who never missed an opportunity to ingratiate herself with anyone with even a modicum of fame, had come smartly into the room as soon as she overheard the words 'MP'.

'Can we get you both some coffee?' she asked.

'How very kind,' said Tim Renfrew. 'Black, two sugars, please.'

Tansy and Holly went through to the kitchen.

'I hope Mum hurries up,' said Holly. 'I'm not into all this polite conversation stuff.'

She poured boiling water on to the coffee and carried the tray through to the lounge.

'My mum won't be long,' she said again.

She had better not be. She felt very awkward standing here.

'Want some juice, William?' she asked, turning round.

There was no sign of William.

'William? Tansy, where's William?'

10.30 a.m. With her heart in her mouth
Holly felt sick. Her heart was pounding in her chest and her legs had turned to water. The front door had been left open. William was nowhere to be seen.

Holly rushed down the front drive, calling his name at the top of her voice. The gate was open and she looked frantically up and down the road, but there was no sign of the little boy. She flew back through the side gate and into the back garden, closely followed by Tansy.

'He can't have gone far,' Tansy said encouragingly. 'He's only little.'

'I know,' sobbed Holly. 'And if anything has happened to him it will all be my fault.'

They looked all round the back garden and then Tansy spotted the gap in the fence. The same thought crossed their minds – building sites were no place for a toddler.

Holly pushed through the gap in the fence, closely followed by Tansy.

'Look!' said Holly urgently.

Outside one of the half-built houses, a large lady in a pair of black leggings and a red sweater was squatting down on her haunches, talking to William and holding his hand. Then she picked him up in her arms and turned towards the road.

'Stop it! Stop!' Holly rushed across the broken bricks and building debris littering what had once been their vegetable garden. 'Put him down!'

The woman turned.

'That's my nephew!' said Holly, remembering all the stories of attempted kidnap that she had ever read. 'Give him to me.'

The woman handed him over, smiling broadly.

'Doddy,' said William.

'Oh my dear, I meant him no harm,' said the

woman. 'I was just afraid he would get hurt – there's broken glass and all sorts of stuff round here. You really should keep a better eye on him, you know.'

Holly glared at her. She felt guilty enough without this woman reading the riot act.

'Doddy,' said William.

'What's he saying?' asked the woman, attempting to break the icy atmosphere.

'Nothing,' said Holly. 'Good morning.'

10.45 a.m. Thank heavens for little boys

'The parents – they're back!' said Holly, as they led a giggling William back into the house. 'If they see William covered in mud, I'll really be for it. You take him upstairs and clean him up, Tansy, and I'll do the charming daughter bit.'

When she went into the sitting room, she found her father sitting in an armchair, his bandaged foot resting on a footstool, trying not to look bored as Tim Renfrew talked politics. Mrs Vine was pouring sherry from a cut-glass decanter and looking rather pink and Leo was sitting on the windowsill looking mildly amused.

'How's the foot, Dad? Anything I can do to help, Mum?'

The bell rang yet again. This place, thought Holly, is getting more like a railway station every day.

Serena and Richard were standing on the doorstep, holding hands and looking all dewy-eyed and soppy.

'We've come for William,' said Serena. 'Where is my little precious lambkin?'

On cue, Tansy came down the stairs, holding a sparklingly clean little lambkin by the hand.

'Who's Mummy's darling boy then?' cooed Serena.

'Tarky Doddy, Mamma,' said William.

'Did William see a doggy then?' murmured Serena, who apparently had a degree in baby talk.

Holly looked at Tansy.

Tansy looked at Holly.

'Come in and have a sherry, darlings,' called Mrs Vine, anxious to portray herself as the together mother-in-law.

'It might not be that doddy – I mean dog,' said Tansy to Holly.

'And we can't make the same mistake twice,' said Holly.

'But then again . . .'

They sped upstairs.

10.55 a.m.

'Hi, Scott. Holly here. We really do think your dog is round here somewhere . . . No, no, I'm not, honestly. William says he saw a dog . . . William?

My brother's kid . . . No, no it's not a wind up –
really I –'

'He's hung up,' said Holly.

'It probably wasn't his dog, anyway,' said
Tansy. 'I mean, babies yabber on about anything,
don't they?'

Holly marched into the sitting room and
squatted down beside William who was system-
atically eating the *Radio Times*.

'Where's the doggy?' she demanded, oblivious
to the astonished gaze of her parents and their
guests.

'Doddy,' said William, smiling beatifically.

'Where?' repeated Holly. 'In the garden? In
your book?'

'Doddy sleeping,' said William. 'Dirty doddy.'

'Good boy!' yelled Holly. 'Come on, Tansy.'

They rushed from the room.

Mrs Vine smiled nervously at her MP.

'The young,' she cooed. 'So vibrant, so full of
life. Have another sherry.'

11 a.m.
The girls pushed their way back through the
fence.

'He must have seen the dog and followed it,'
reasoned Tansy. 'So it has to be here somewhere.'

They peered into the first of the half-built
houses.

'We ought to go in and look,' suggested Holly.

They were just climbing through the unfinished doorway when they heard a whimper.

'Listen!' said Tansy.

They heard it again.

In the hole that would one day be a stylish fireplace lay Fitz. He was damp, very muddy and one paw was crusted with blood. He raised his head and stared dolefully at the two girls.

'It's him!' breathed Holly. 'We've found him. Give me a blanket.'

Tansy pulled a face.

'Oh yes, building sites are awash with freshly laundered bedding,' she said. 'Here, take this.'

She slipped her arms out of her denim jacket and handed it to Holly who tenderly picked up the whimpering dog in her arms.

'You can see', she said, looking at its liquid-brown eyes, 'why Scott loves him so much.'

Tansy smiled.

'Now all we have to do is tell him how you risked life and limb to rescue him, and maybe he'll love you too,' she said.

I wish, thought Holly.

11.10 a.m.

When Holly, closely followed by Tansy, carried Fitz into the sitting room, she found her mother

127

and father and Tim Renfrew sitting coyly on the sofa, while Leo aimed a camera at them.

'Just one more!' he said, squatting on his haunches. 'Terrific, absolutely terrific.'

Holly's mother turned her gaze on her daughter, and her mouth fell open.

'Holly dear, what on earth is that?' she said.

Holly went through the whole saga again and Leo clapped his hands in delight.

'Amazing!' he said. 'The theme continues – "The Vine Family: Champions of the Underdog". I love it! What a headline!'

It is, thought Holly, an improvement on the 'Roundhead and the Rabbit'.

'Get into the picture, Holly – with the little dog.'

Holly shook her head.

'I've got to get him back to Scott,' she began. 'He won't believe me if I phone.'

'Why not?'

'It's too complicated to explain,' said Holly hastily.

'OK, do the pic and I'll phone him,' he said. 'People believe reporters.'

'Not all of them,' commented the MP dryly.

Noon. Things get better
Scott was down on his knees hugging Fitz and trying to hide the tears in his eyes.

'Thanks, Holly,' he said, his voice muffled as he

pressed his face into Fitz's grubby coat. 'Sorry I didn't believe you.'

'It's OK,' said Holly. 'I don't blame you. Don't you think you should take him to the vet?'

Scott nodded.

'My dad's outside with the car – I'll take him now. Can you let Jade know we've found Fitz? She's been brilliant.'

Holly sighed.

'Yes,' she said. 'Of course I will.'

'Thanks again,' said Scott with a grin and Holly's battered heart did another lurch.

'Don't worry,' whispered Tansy as Scott drove off with his dad. 'There are plenty more guys where he came from.'

Maybe, thought Holly. But they don't seem to be falling over themselves to get to me.

'Right, Angela, so that's all agreed, is it?' said Tim Renfrew, downing the last of his sherry and standing up. 'You'll get me all the details and I'll take this matter up in the House. It's too important to sweep under the carpet.'

'Of course, Tim, and thank you,' Mrs Vine purred.

'Oh no, thank *you*,' said the MP. He turned to Holly. 'You must be very proud of your mother – one day I hope we'll see her on the benches. This country needs more people like her. People who really care.'

Yes, thought Holly, she does care, doesn't she? And not just about other people. She really does care about me.

She'll probably know what to do about the boobs.

1 p.m.

Mrs Vine was in the kitchen singing. It was not something she was good at, but Holly was so relieved to have her mother in a good mood that she put up with her unique rendition of 'Don't Cry For Me Argentina'.

'Are you staying for lunch, Tansy dear?' she asked, chopping carrots with ferocious determination.

Tansy shook her head.

'I'd love to,' she said, 'but Mum said I had to go home. She's got that awful Laurence coming for lunch – he's enough to put anyone off their food.'

Mrs Vine laughed.

'I'm sure he can't be that bad, Tansy,' she said. 'Not if your mum likes him.'

'She is', commented Tansy dryly, 'very easily pleased.'

She picked up her jacket and rucksack and beamed at Mrs Vine.

'Thank you very much for having me,' she said. 'Bye, Holly!'

A thought crossed Holly's mind.

'Hang on,' she said. 'I'll walk to the end of the road with you.'

'Hey,' said Tansy. 'You're going the wrong way.'

'I'm not really going to walk with you, stupid,' said Holly.

'Charming,' said Tansy mildly. 'Where are you going then?'

Holly took a deep breath.

'I was completely out of order last night,' she admitted. 'I'm going to set things straight with Scott. No, it's OK,' she added as Tansy opened her mouth. 'I know Jade and him are an item; I just want to say I'm sorry.'

'Good on you,' said Tansy.

1.20 p.m. Taking a very deep breath

The door of Scott's house was opened by a large lady with jet-black hair and an unrestrained bosom. From inside came the sound of noisy laughter and glasses clinking.

'Is Scott in?' Holly asked nervously.

'But of course,' the woman beamed. 'Scott! Scott!'

Scott appeared from the kitchen.

'Thanks, Gran,' he said. 'Hi, Holly. Excuse the noise – it's my uncle's birthday. They're drinking Chianti and being utterly stupid.'

Holly breathed a sigh of relief. Scott sounded quite normal with her.

'Look,' she began hastily, 'I am really sorry about lying to you yesterday. Can we still be friends?'

'Of course,' said Scott. 'I like you a lot. You're a good mate, really you are.'

That, thought Holly, is enough for me. For now at any rate.

3 p.m. A newcomer with possibilities

Halfway through Sunday lunch, the doorbell shrilled.

'Oh no,' sighed Mrs Vine. 'What now?'

'I'll get it,' said her husband. 'I've got to get used to these crutches.' He hobbled to the door and returned with the woman Holly had shouted at on the building site.

'Hello again,' she chirruped, smiling at Holly. 'So sorry to intrude but I found this after you had gone.' She held up an exceedingly mangy blue toy elephant. 'I think the little lad –'

'Thank you so much,' gasped Holly, snatching the toy. 'Isn't it odd what strange things dogs play with?'

Please don't mention William, she prayed. I can't stand getting into any more trouble.

'Let me introduce myself,' the woman continued to Holly's relief. 'I'm Deannie Bennett, and I'm

132

going to be your new neighbour. Over the back –
the house on the left.'

'How charming!' said Mr Vine politely, hoping
she would go so that he could get on with his roast
pork.

'It's perfect for my tribe,' she said. 'Our bunga-
low in Ridgeway is far too small for three
teenagers.'

'You have children then,' said Mr Vine, praying
they would be of the quiet variety.

'Kirsty's thirteen, and the twins are fifteen,' she
said. 'Honestly, who'd have teenage boys?'

'Me,' said Holly without thinking. And everyone
laughed.

9 p.m. Making up

By nine o'clock Mr Vine had retired to bed to rest
his aching foot and Holly and her mum were
sitting in the kitchen drinking hot chocolate
and stuffing themselves with coconut cookies.

'Mum,' Holly began, suddenly feeling very shy
and little. 'Can I ask you something?'

'Of course you can, sweetheart,' her mother
assured her. 'What is it?'

Holly took a deep breath.

'The thing is, what I'm trying to say is . . . one of
my boobs is bigger than the other.'

She chewed her lip.

'Oh, darling, isn't it irritating when that

happens!' cried her mother, as if commenting on a cake that had failed to rise. 'Mine were totally out of kilter when I was your age. It's no big deal – but if it bothers you, we'll see the doctor, just to put your mind at rest.'

She paused.

'I'm sorry, Holly, really I am,' she said.

'What for?' asked Holly in surprise.

Her mother sighed.

'Well, I've been so keen on giving you personal space and privacy – and maybe I overdid it. I don't know – after the boys, I was so thrilled to have a daughter that I was determined not to blow it by becoming an over-protective mum.'

'Were you?' interrupted Holly. 'Were you really thrilled to have me?'

'Darling, of course I was. I just wish I had known that you were worrying – then we could have sorted it all out sooner.'

Holly hugged her mother.

'That's OK,' she said. 'Everything's sorted now.'

Want to find out
what happens to
the girls in
another great
What a Week story?

Then sneak a peek
over the page ...

'Hi, Tansy – guess what?' Holly Vine was hopping up and down on one leg in excitement, her nutmeg-brown hair flopping over her face.

'You're in love again?' suggested Tansy. She knew that Holly's main aim in life was to get a guy and, generally speaking, when her friend was in high spirits a boy was involved somewhere.

'No, silly – although one of the boys who are going to be moving into the new house behind us is to die for.'

Cleo and Tansy exchanged 'here we go again' glances and grinned.

'No,' continued Holly excitedly, 'it's even better than that! You know *Go For It!* – that TV game show on Saturday mornings?'

Tansy nodded. *GFI!* was one of the coolest shows for teens on cable – everyone watched it, partly because of Ben Bolter, the dishy presenter, and partly because it was so wickedly off the wall and different from any other show on TV.

'Go on,' urged Cleo. 'Tell her.'

'Well,' began Holly, savouring her role as bringer of great tidings. 'They're coming to Dunchester. For Saturday's show! And West Green Upper's going to be one of the schools taking part!'

Tansy's eyes widened in disbelief.

'You're kidding!' she breathed. 'How do you know? No one ever knows.'

What made *GFI!* so different from anything else

on TV was its unpredictability. Schools wrote in for a chance to send a team of kids, but it wasn't until the week of the live show that they got to know whether they had been picked.

Go For It! was all about ambition and making dreams come true. It had Go for Cash, Go for Glory and Go for the Top rounds, and if your team got through to the final round, you each got to Go for IT – your own personal dream. The prizes were ace, and the whole thing was brilliant viewing. To take part, thought Tansy, would be the funkiest thing ever.

'Isn't it great?' said Cleo, hitching her rucksack over her shoulder as the school bus came round the corner. 'Who do you reckon will get on the team?'

Me, if I have anything to do with it, thought Tansy, her brain whirring as she imagined being spotted by a talent scout and whisked off to a life of indulgence on a film set in Beverly Hills. This could be my passport to fame.

From *What a Week to Make it Big* – available now!

What a Week

to Make it Big

by Rosie Rushton

There's huge excitement when the girls find out that a cable-TV quiz show is coming to their school. This is their big chance to be on TV and get a taste of fame – as well as meet the *very* gorgeous presenter.

But not everyone can make it big. Being left out and suffering from an attack of the green-eyed monster is no fun at all. It's at times like this than you find out who your *real* friends are ...

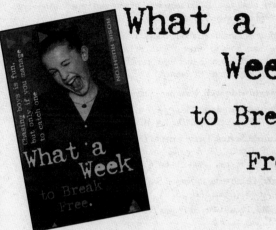

What a Week
to Break
Free

by Rosie Rushton

The school activity weekend is coming up and everyone's got big plans – which don't include the organized activities. Canoeing, abseiling and mountain biking are all very well but there are more important things to consider – like boys ...

Poor Jade, however, is in serious trouble. She desperately needs to get away from her so-called 'home' and start a new life. But can she carry off her plans?

READ MORE IN PUFFIN

For children of all ages, Puffin represents quality and variety – the very best in publishing today around the world.

For complete information about books available from Puffin – and Penguin – and how to order them, contact us at the appropriate address below. Please note that for copyright reasons the selection of books varies from country to country.

On the worldwide web: www.penguin.com

In the United Kingdom: Please write to *Dept. EP, Penguin Books Ltd, Bath Road, Harmondsworth, West Drayton, Middlesex UB7 0DA*

In the United States: Please write to *Consumer Sales, Penguin USA, P.O. Box 999, Dept. 17109, Bergenfield, New Jersey 07621-0120*. VISA and MasterCard holders call 1-800-253-6476 to order Penguin titles

In Canada: Please write to *Penguin Books Canada Ltd, 10 Alcorn Avenue, Suite 300, Toronto, Ontario M4V 3B2*

In Australia: Please write to *Penguin Books Australia Ltd, P.O. Box 257, Ringwood, Victoria 3134*

In New Zealand: Please write to *Penguin Books (NZ) Ltd, Private Bag 102902, North Shore Mail Centre, Auckland 10*

In India: Please write to *Penguin Books India Pvt Ltd, 706 Eros Apartments, 56 Nehru Place, New Delhi 110 019*

In the Netherlands: Please write to *Penguin Books Netherlands bv, Postbus 3507, NL-1001 AH Amsterdam*

In Germany: Please write to *Penguin Books Deutschland GmbH, Metzlerstrasse 26, 60594 Frankfurt am Main*

In Spain: Please write to *Penguin Books S. A., Bravo Murillo 19, 1° B, 28015 Madrid*

In Italy: Please write to *Penguin Italia s.r.l., Via Felice Casati 20, I–20124 Milano*

In France: Please write to *Penguin France S. A., 17 rue Lejeune, F–31000 Toulouse*

In Japan: Please write to *Penguin Books Japan, Ishikiribashi Building, 2–5–4, Suido, Bunkyo-ku, Tokyo 112*

In South Africa: Please write to *Longman Penguin Southern Africa (Pty) Ltd, Private Bag X08, Bertsham 2013*